W. F Hobson

Catharine Leslie Hobson, Lady-Nurse, Crimean War, and Her Life

W. F Hobson

Catharine Leslie Hobson, Lady-Nurse, Crimean War, and Her Life

ISBN/EAN: 9783337119768

Printed in Europe, USA, Canada, Australia, Japan

Cover: Foto ©Raphael Reischuk / pixelio.de

More available books at **www.hansebooks.com**

Catharine Leslie Hobson,

LADY-NURSE, CRIMEAN WAR,

AND

HER LIFE.

BY THE

REV. W. F. HOBSON, M.A.,

St. Catharine's College, Cambridge ;
Author of "Science and Faith;" "Sacerdotalism;"
"Vestments and Law;" "Church Innovations;"
"Church Reform," etc.

"All Kates are Cates."—*Shakespeare.*

Parker and Co.

6 SOUTHAMPTON-STREET, STRAND, LONDON ;

AND BROAD-STREET, OXFORD.

1888.

PREFACE.

—✠—

I AM sensible of much deficiency in this little book, and it may be said that a work needing excuse had better not appear. Nevertheless, though conceived and mostly written in bed, "in the cloud and in the sea" of an uncommon visitation, and afterwards whilst long "stumbling on the dark mountains" of heavy oppression, I trust that the divine ideal of a life and character will over-shine the defects of the poor human limner.

W. F. HOBSON.

Temple Ewell,
October, 1888.

ERRATA.

Page 8, line 14 from top, *for* '*mauvaise quatre heure*' *read* '*mauvais quart d'heure.*'

Page 34, line 4 from bottom, *for* 'Retcliffe's' *read* 'Redcliffe's.'

Page 52, *read* 3rd line from bottom as a fresh line of text.

Catharine Leslie Hobson.

✠

CHAPTER I.

"Thou madest man, he knows not why."—*Tennyson.*

"What am I, and whence come I . . . . ?"—*Cowper.*

"Thou hast no star upon thy brow
Young heritor of time. . . ."—*Mrs. Harvey.*

"FAR be it from me to pass unmoved by any spot made memorable by virtue, or consecrated by religion. The man is little to be envied whose patriotism would not gain strength on the plains of Marathon, or whose piety would not grow warm amid the ruins of Iona." Johnson's sentiment is so human and natural that no one will question it, unless it be some who have parted with religion, dispensed with God, and dug up, with scientific spud, the very root of morals — making virtue an open question, and vice of such near kin that both are indifferent; or others who, superstitious against superstition, regard Iona's relics as only a monument of the " Dark Ages," now to be despised as wholly *bad.* Nevertheless some distinction *is* made still,

B

and noble daring and good deeds are yet praised
for their own sakes, and for the benefits they confer
upon humanity : but, alas ! the impressions of noblest
deeds of heroism grow faint in the haze of time ; and
disinterested services of pure devotion and self-denial
are too soon lost sight of in the gross, absorbing race
of self-interest. The martyr Gordon, and saint of
God, how swiftly he was in oblivion with the men
who had been the cause of his fall ; and the glory
of such a Christian and Soldier story was denied its
due memorial in the crush of political and party
necessities : even Mr. Gladstone could say, "We
have heard enough of Kartoum ;" but hearts of flesh
will yet believe that "'tis not so above."   Against
the scientist's solvents of morality, and against the
world's incredulity of goodness, I venture to say—

> Go, soul ! the body's guest,
>   Upon a thankless errand ;
> Obey my high behest
>   And give the world the lie.

Yet it was not without hesitation, and some fear,
that I determined, at the bidding of a secret voice,
to try, with weak hand and enfeebled frame, to draw
out the figure of character which follows ; and, " lean-
ing on the cross with aspect sad," to add one more
appeal to Johnson's thought ; one more witness for

God ; in the only desire to confirm those who yet believe in virtue, goodness, and truth ; justified, I hope, by the conviction that this life-statue is of value for the living. I may be in error, but I stand on my own conscience ; and, as to success, I surely account one individual soul's benefit—if God may grant that to me—infinitely beyond the bookseller's receipts or the bookstall's doubtful notoriety.

The lines that follow were penned in 1856, while yet two lives, becoming one, might have been severed for ever. They were addressed to her of whom this little record will say something more, presenting glimpses, too scanty and partial, of a life that afterwards for thirty-two years was one with my own in never-ceasing love, and with a bright shining of unselfish goodness on all around.

> Go ! on thy upward way,
>   Thou dearest name on earth ;
> For me no longer stay ;
>   For one so little worth.
>
> Go ! onward, upward, higher,
>   Still in the life divine ;
> And me, till flood and fire
>   Shall purify, resign.
>
> It may be, never more
>   Our paths, on earth, shall meet ;
> Self-sacrifice before
>   Appears—for either meet.

Not long, not long, the time !
Till both made perfect, we
Heavenward in Christ shall climb,
In Him each other see.

Out of SIGĒ, 'silence,' very early heretics feigned, with fervid fancy, that all things were brought forth : the word was a power, shadowing all hidden mysteries, but *why* anything ever came out of that cloud, none might answer : they left the insoluble puzzle of creation and of man unsolved. JOB was more concerned with the "why" than with the source of his life, and questioned, "*Why* died I not from the womb?" "I should have slept : then had I been at rest, with kings and counsellors of the earth."

Why was any human *Soul* brought out of silence into the unrest, discord, toil and sorrow of a mortal life ? Has matter, of itself, a purpose and a reason, in a sphere beyond its own powers ? believe it not ; it is a great mystery, before which man is dumb; yea even angels' thought may never have swept the infinite of a divine reason ; but the *deed* is done, and doing; and it is of such unutterable vastness, if rightly grasped, whether it be by the slow becoming of evolution or otherwise, that no wonder if harpers harp with golden harps before the fountain of being on each such projection from the SIGĒ, and make some record of the *deed.* But if the outward first appearing of the Soul be worthy of record, how may not the whole record be kept also in a "Book of Life?" Every life, as every particle of matter, has a secret *Cosmic* relation ; and if the issues of good and evil are immeasurable, enduring for ages past and future, life has a normal title to be related. Men tell the stories of general history, and the marvels of their own handiwork—"the gorgeous palaces, the solemn temples," their rivalry even with nature in some vast design, and wonder rightly at such things ; and yet, as Gibbon says of Justinian's boast over *Santa Sophia*[*], "How dull is the artifice, how insignificant is the labour, if it be compared with the formation of the vilest insect that crawls upon the surface of the temple !" But how infinitely more, beyond comparison, is a rational human Soul ! yea, even the sun or moon or any star is not so divine a *deed* as that.

> "Onward and ever onward shalt thou fling
> Eternity around thee. . . ."—*I. Williams.*

[*] "Solomon, I have vanquished thee."

CHAPTER II.

—✠—

"I could have laughed myself to scorn to find
In that decrepid man so firm a mind."

"The child is father of the man."—*Wordsworth.*

I HAVE often and often admired how the meek
things of the earth justify themselves, all unconsciously, even before the great ones of the world,
just by being what they *are* in self-forgetfulness;
each one having some individual quality which
others potently feel and confess, whilst they themselves are liable to miss its force. They cannot be
unfaithful to it, for it is the mere unconscious self-
action of their true life. The power of self-assertion
in the "weak things" of the world, without self-
estimation or personal aim, is charming in animals,
in its perfect naturalness and absence of show; no
false attitude; no concealment; the grandest *pose* of
horse or dog is put on and thrown off with equally
unconscious ease. But of all the things that share
the earth with harsh and selfish man, in its singular
weakness and frailty, a flower is unsurpassed in its

grace of self-assertion. Look at that pansy, or that yellow primrose; the presence of a mighty king is not more assured, more strangely and witchingly *calm*, with a royalty that is of Nature; and so the " wee modest crimson-tippèd flower " stands erect and assured as an armed man empanoplied in steel.

Such thoughts of calm self-hood are imaged in the memory of the life of her whom I tremblingly have chosen to sketch briefly. A character without repose is radically defective—" peace is the tranquillity of liberty," and repose the proportional of action. An intensity of activity, hidden by a fixed and deep repose from a stranger's eye, required a daily observation to understand; but it made a sweet harmony to those who saw the habitual proof of both : nay ! it were not a paradox to say that her hours of repose were laborious, and her days of labour were rest. But never was there any strain at self-assertion; only the self-possessing reality, the " earnest " *doing*, for its own sake, of what the day brought forth. Her very body in walking partook of the quality here noted; as the son of Sirach says, " A man is known by his gait." She moved in a balanced progress, with rythmical action and an all unconscious stateliness of tread, which few attain; for walking is not really an everyday feat, performed

by all; and is too often travestied by a shuffle, a
jerk, a hop, a swing, or some other peculiarity that
is not real walking; nor was this the result of effort;
her eyes would be "far away," her thoughts pre-
occupied, and by the mere force of habit

> "She walked in beauty like the night
> Of cloudless climes and starry skies."

The charm never deserted her. Ordering for more
than twenty years large public sales of charitable
work, with ever so many lady-helpers, she was ever the
one head, referred to by everybody in any difficulty;
she never knew flurry; was never disturbed; and it
was the same in the presence of danger. I once had
a *mauvaise quatre heure* on the rapid Bosphorus by
Therapia. There, as on the Sea of Galilee, sudden
squalls spring up instantaneously, rushing down the
deep gorges on either side of the bright sea-river.
We were in a *caïque*, frailest of frail craft. It was
single-oared, with one Turk only, and the rush of
the storm brake like a broadside; the waves jumped
madly; the boat tossed like a cork before the wild
wind, and, as was his wont, the fatalist boatman suddenly threw down his oars and all seemed lost; every
second might be the hopeless upset: to get at the
oar or manage the *caïque* was impossible. I feared
to look at the face beside me, but, at last, one glance

was enough. With unblanched cheek and not a sign of fear, she sat calm and silent, only once smiling at the poor fatalist. The storm, as usual, went by as quickly as it burst, and I recovered from my panic.

Character is often traced back to early childhood by the loving partiality of parents. They may sometimes note trivial things, and some things whose significance is dubious, or only of interest to relatives, or clearly not to the point, but enough remains of undoubted certainty to prove that some qualities are so early manifested in certain individuals as to show that later developments are not mere accidents, but are a pure strain of nature. My vital statue, while yet a girl (aged 14), had a girl friend who had to have an operation for tumour in the breast, but who resolutely resisted unless "Kate" might hold her hand all the time. This she did, the doctor telling her that if she flinched, or moved, or sickened, the greatest mischief would ensue. The hand *was* held, without a tremour or shrinking, lovingly, steadily, calmly. The operation succeeded, and then the operator said quickly, "Hold out your hand," and *he put the tumour into "Kate's" hand!* Another doctor present remonstrated, and was answered, "She showed such pluck that I thought I would see how far she could go!"

The seeming opposites of feminine delicacy and weakness, coincident with stoic immoveableness and hardy endurance, are not incredible; the sternest and most rigid face I ever knew was that of a man most sensitive to the ridiculous, and whose looks were only the sign of the fierce self-restraint put upon his natural temperament, as he thought due to his office, he being a clergyman. So one of the finest operators of modern days was sensitive to excess, and pitiful in the extreme, but, with a patient under his knife, he said he knew no feeling, no relenting.

CHAPTER III.

—✠—

"... and departing leave behind us
Footprints on the sands of time,
Footprints which perhaps another
Sailing o'er life's solemn main,
Some forlorn and shipwrecked brother
Seeing may take heart again."—*Longfellow.*

WHAT justifies a "book of life," however briefly written? It is not as a portrait, which a man procures from mere fashion, and with little motive often, unless to see what is his own image "as others see him." The *book* is for others, written generally only when a man has begun to "know even as he is known," and there ought to be solid motive for the work: mere private affection is insufficient; an evident aim to subserve a cause by a "Life" is a defect; mere worldly station, noble birth or old historic heritage, are invalid or incomplete motives; even intellectual power is not always worth record[a]. A

---

[a] A recent life of Lady Georgiana Fullerton (from the French) by a Jesuit, H. J. Coleridge, as he has written or rewritten it, seems to me thus to lack justification, as it therefore needed *much* padding: in fact it is padded out of all proportion, so as to remind one of the story of Sheridan who, on repeating from his part "drip, drip, drip," suddenly exclaimed, "Why bless

life should contain actual life, not its mere accidents, or one solitary unused or abused gift.   Character, and

my soul, there's nought but '*dripping*' here !" and so damned a Tragedy of S. T. Coleridge ! the padding, too, is not of the best ; and most of the letters of so gifted a woman are remarkably without her higher qualities of thought and subject.   One feels also from the first page onward, as suddenly dropped into an *entourage* of coronets—specially such as were "converts,"— social dignities, draperies of fashion, and secular "powers that be," with some 59 *pages* of domestic trivialities and ordinary child and girl life, "when Georgiana finally left the school-room !"   Ask for the justification of such a "life," and there is little or nothing definite and in detail, imitable or uncommon.   The only patent explanation of the book is (and in this light it is skilfully managed and "cooked up" for weak-kneed Anglicans) that its subject was the author of some striking and charming novels ; and became a Romanist ; *how* one is not directly told, though it appears to have been by the gradual drifting of a gentle soul, under a life-long sensitiveness of the "sinfulness of sin;" the loud and tempting lure of perfect absolution, always promised by Rome ; her husband's example ; the special attraction to her of the scenic grandeur of the Romish Church, its music and ritual, from childhood ; and, above all, as with other deserters, a too superficial grounding in and grasp of the true catholic element and spirit of the English Church, resulting in a " commonplace" religion, of weak avail against opposing attractions.   She wanted something more real and spiritual than the religion around her.   The "conversion " is but too suggestive as the central spring, and fly-wheel, of the book.   Of *action*, essential to the ideal of a written record, there is no proper force or variety : like many another talented novel writer—especially among women authors—Lady Georgiana's exterior life was

notable action, some quality or gift resulting in imitable effect upon. other lives, claim a primary record in earthly story ; the moral mould of an individual rather than the mere mental cast; the spiritual before the material or secular capacity. Of course I am not here speaking of the world's estimate or standard but of a higher one. Moreover, the record, above all else, should be in the very spirit of truth, referring to and sustained by facts : a " Robinson Crusoe " may entertain, but it can never be a witness or be appealed to on the moral side : as the Confessions of S. Augustine, so should the record of a " life " be — the true presentation of its subject by his or her own words, as far as possible, or at least the genuine evidence of

mainly as the ordinary routine of her high station, at least until her "conversion ; " and as to events had nothing to distinguish it, in itself, from a thousand others ; whilst the interior, intrinsically interesting, was almost a secret ; albeit that interior, without worldly trappings, was what alone had a *right* to be written in a book. The repeated but obscure hints and vague references to matters not detailed, and to " good works "—of course after conversion—as requiring a " whole volume " to contain them, and not even to be " catalogued " for their number, are but poor bricks wherewith to build up a literary " house of life." All this I venture to say, not in want of any regard to a good, gifted, beneficent and holy woman and author —valued exceedingly in our house—but simply as a fair comment on a literary work and illustrative of the question of the text.

one having access to the truth, with all available corroborative facts and action. It is a specially difficult and delicate task (or so I have felt) for a husband, or wife, to be a biographer of the other, and to tell all wholesome truth, unwarped by partiality, and, from their nearness to each other, to avoid disproportion and lack of perspective, in the choice of incidents and the outline of the narrative. What affects themselves the most, is not the same as that which may delight or profit others. Incidents, too, of that inward or private life common to both, upon which so much of action and motive depend, are often a sort of sacred preserve, the veil of which none may remove. But there is a real sense in which every life *belongs* not to ourselves but to others; " No one liveth to himself and no one dieth to himself" has a human as well as the divine side. Of a "life," that may manifestly be of use to others, there is an aspect of *obligation* to give the presentation of it, more or less fully; and in this thought, supremely, I decided to write or sculpture my statue, and so—

" Go forth now my little book."—*Bunyan.*

There were two Misses Anderson prepared for hospital work, who went together, and became friends, in 1854 to the then nearly untried career of Lady-nurses, about which " some doubted," and many more were amazed, until, by saintly ministries and the touch of a sister's or mother's pitying hand, was won for ever the blessing of the suffering and dying soldiers, in that time of horrors ; never since repeated ; for the new devotion and usefulness of Holy Women made the Order of "The Red Cross" and others, sisters and men, to become a blessed part of the re-gular provision of an army in all the civilized world.

"So far a good deed shines in a naughty world."—*Shakespeare.*

It was in truth the spring-time of a great outburst of Devotion and Charity to that Lord who " bare our sicknesses ; " and the homes of Christian England were widely moved with patriot and Christian zeal, so that many a daughter of the land—a " one ewe lamb " — offered herself willingly to the sacrifice. Women of gentle birth came forward as eagerly as their poorer sisters, who could only offer themselves as hired servants ; and when once at Kululi [b] a revolt of the latter sprang up against the patients' washing, a lady, fresh from the Queen's Court, stood up to the work of the common wash-tub, and by her, whilst at work or sitting to rest awhile, many a sly contrast

[b] This spelling is given as nearest to the pronunciation on the spot, the ' i ' sounded ' e.'

of conditions was thrown off *sotto voce* to " Miss Kate :"
" It's as hot as a summer drawing-room ; " "without
the grand dresses ; " "and the crowded rooms," and
so on.

There was room for all helpers, and need of more.
Some were *trained* and competent, others had to
stumble on as best they might, and learn by doing.
The first paid nurses had a bad record (see pages 33,
41, 42) ; one got to Constantinople but never nursed
at all, nor ever meant to nurse ; her only motive was
to join her soldier husband at the public expense.
Others did worse with no excuse, and were got rid
of variously. One lady-nurse also innocently brought
a pet lap-dog (which I saw) as part of her outfit for
hospital-work, where pain, disease, and death reigned
rampant ! The *Soul* whom in briefest sketch it is my
choice to discourse of, then Catherine Leslie Anderson, was not of the unready. *Why* she had " burst out
of the silent land" into this work and scenes of harrowing gloom and suffering, might be, in some way,
known by the visible fitness of the living instrument
for the sphere now found for her ; and so with others :
if the Soul was not brought forth *for* the work, there
was work in the wide world always waiting for the
new visitant to Earth's confusing scenes and mysterious complications of life and death, pains and

sorrows ; and if such were not the ultimate *reason* of a life they were as justifying side-lights to the question of Creation's purpose.

That there is a " correspondence " of the invisible to the actual—of the internal state of a soul and the realized experience of life—is a conviction of deep concern ; and that an interior disposition fits and determines our outward way is a great fact ; we all receive "grace for grace," and "every man hath his *proper* gift of God ;" and a soul's chief longing, when it is the outcome of an unselfish devotion, is as a lightning-conductor drawing down celestial force ; yea, it has the direct *promise* of divine response, " He will fulfil the *desire* of them that fear Him." So the call to what we are most fitted for comes surely, and perhaps only once ; which if despised or neglected comes not again—

> "There is a tide in the affairs of men,
> Which, taken at the turn, leads on . . ."

and this is as true in the spiritual as in the outward life. The subject of this sketch was a clear illustration of the truth of the " correspondence " here referred to. She always *desired* to be a helper to others. " Pity (says Johnson) is not natural to man :" if not, it was so early a gift of grace to her as to

c

become a "*second* nature," and she ever found the
work before her that answered her desire, and for
which she was most fitted.

In a volume of MS. poems, copied carefully from
many sources, she has recorded her own life-ideal—

"For it is beautiful only to do the thing we are *meant* for."

This has no name, but the last verse of one of her
own poems is—

"Then only lift Thy Blessed Veil
Just high enough for us to see
That we are walking in the road,
The narrow road that leads to Thee."

The daughter of a Master in the Royal Navy
(a title now disused), she was born at Stoke, Devon-
shire, and baptized in 1823, and from very early
years she had sought in poverty, sickness, and suffering a better occupation and solace for the active
sympathetic mind than in the usual amusements and
gaieties that captivate the young : not that there was
a shade or tinge of despite in her to the innocent
"follies" of the Heart's spring-time. It was only any,
and every, offence against manners or morals that
roused her, and she was ready to rebuke such at
all times, whoever the offender, and often with start-

ling quickness, sharp as the point of a rapier. A
young officer, in her girlish days, was rude to her
and a companion in the streets of Plymouth or
Stoke, and, on some quick word, with a mock apology, inquired if she were speaking to *him;* to which
she calmly replied, " No, it was to that *other* puppy ;"
a young dog being by her side ! A " gentleman "
to her was a name of high honour all her life ; with,
perhaps, some slight partiality for the "naval blue,"
whose real gentlemen are inimitably typical of chival-
ries now, alas ! dying or dead.

The visiting in union-houses—such as they then
were—was not yet accepted as a mission for ladies.
Her first experience was such, working for and with
the parochial clergy, and to this was added the worst
slums of Devonport, by the dockyard. Dread were
her reminiscences of that work in after days—un-
nameable immorality, unshamed vice ; and yet in
the worst localities some pure mother was found
bringing up a family, in a very hotbed of evil, as
" trees which the Lord had planted." Truly the *soul*
of our sister was learning mysteries, and justifying
her own Life !

———✠———

CHAPTER IV

" By reason of use have their senses exercised."—*Heb.* v.

" A man must serve his time to every trade."—*Byron.*

Hamlet.—"I pray you play upon this lute."

Player.—" We cannot, my lord."

NCONSCIOUS and providential preparation —the divine making of an instrument to do future work went on. "Miss Kate" [the name that friends—Miss Stanley, Miss E. Anderson, for memory's sake, and a few others—continued to use even after her marriage] learned the conditions of lonely country life and the *morale* of a village, where a home industry had the blame of shaping the habits and character of the people. The curate with whom she had worked in Devonport went to the Benefice of P——, and a few months later she joined him and his wife to help, and to learn the practical work of instituting church order and parochial ministrations where such had for years and years been unknown, or had lapsed. The straw-plaiting industry was universal thereabouts; it was as the order of nature to the villagers. Every one was, of course, a plaiter—young men, women, and children. The work, from morn till eve and every working-day, was done in every place; in the house, in the fields, in the hedge-bottoms, and all covert corners, out of sight. Only the *hands* were needed to plait, the mind and tongue were unloosed ; and the latter "unruly member" was an "unruly evil, setting on fire the course of *nature*" in young growing girls, boys, and budding manhood and womanhood. Everywhere were sauntering groups or pairs ; others would be sitting or lying about the lanes all day long; only missed during the brief pause for meals. Every soul born was a plaiter; a straw was the child's first plaything, and is so still, teaching by its habitual handling a facility of manipulation which would only be gained by making the poor little ones, from the cradle, the very slaves of the straw. It was worse even than the "stich, stitch, stitch" of the needlewomen of the great city, for the very infant that "knew not good or evil" was here its earlier victim. "Miss Kate" was moved with pity and indignation, and in verse and prose showed her abhorence of the evil :—

> Little hands, whose hardest labour
> Should be weaving daisy-chains,
> Aye are toiling at this plaiting,
> Adding to their mother's gains :

Little voices that should warble
  Blithely as the summer bird,
Here by harsh control you still them,
  Childish melody unheard.

The evil results of the trade were manifold. Even in the school (such as it then was) the plaiting went on. Classes of boys and girls, when their hands were not engaged, plaited all day long, and the abounding joyousness of young hearts had its *time* for playful expression grudged and repressed. The sad revenge of outraged nature commonly appeared in the escape of mere children from home and parental control, and in the curse of perfect independence of the young of both sexes. Home authority was scarcely known when mere children could support themselves by plaiting; and houses were everywhere for children-*lodgers*, as for adults! For any, or no cause the home circle was left, and an ever open door received the runaway to the companionship of those who had done the same thing; there was no general attempt to put down the vicious habit; nor had any difficulty or hindrance or any reproach to be overcome by the erring ones. The effects of such a social state were foulest moral corruption; girls knew no chastity, boys no fear or restraint; illegitimacy was the most usual birth, and there was no shame to young mothers or fathers : the baptismal register was avoided ; the rite of Holy Matrimony was a mere *legal* form and a matter of choice, as each one fancied. The clergy non-resident for unknown years ; the ancient house of prayer dilapidated, and no spiritual work outside, nor any civilizing social influence available. A more saddening, moral sore ; a less hopeful condition for a soul than these plaiting villages exhibited it is hardly possible to imagine ; the evil was appalling, the remedy super-human, and yet, O " lukewarm hearts," *that* work which seemed so paralyzing to contemplate, has been done—someway at least—and by one clergyman alone, whose initiatory steps were shared and helped by " Miss Kate ; " until the loud cry of a more widespread, harrowing calamity rent the sky and moved man and woman from ordinary home ministries to the far-off battle-field, and the alike fatal war-hospitals. To her and to myself the call was simultaneous ; she was moved by the harrowing accounts of suffering and hardships, and I, on the first death of a chaplain of cholera at Balaklava, volunteered to take his place ; and so two souls in their several orbits, unknown to each other, were being drawn into conjunction by the mysterious interworkings of a divine, world-ruling purpose.

Of her work at P—— the still living sharer with
her writes : " We worked together to clothe and
humanize rough country people, whom we found
with little religion and less morality ; and her nimble
fingers made boys' caps and girls' clothes out of any
material we could get, and there are many still living
who remember Miss Anderson. . . . . . She taught
in the Sunday-school, visited, and in every way
assisted us . . . . . . and she more than once took
rags off the children and put on them decent clothing, even if to be *made out of some of her own.*"

When the nurses were chosen each one was for
a time trained in a London hospital, under the
doctors in charge, in the practical services of carry-
ing out their orders, with such additional instruction
in various matters, bandaging and other manipula-
tions of the sick and wounded, as under direction
or in a sudden emergency might be done by sisters ;
and here previous experience and some special skill
of hand caused " Miss Kate " to excel and be *first*
in the surgeon's certificate.

What a marvel the human hand is ! Some hands
are formless and veinless, lumps of flesh, and little
more. Here is her individual hand, but not till
work had told upon it, and strain upon strain had

.t

A cutting out of large Photograph, 1861.

started the muscles into knots, and enlarged greatly
the forefinger, which for many years became almost
helpless, sadly painful, and at last useless.   Once
it was amply veined, with nervous long fingers, deli-
cate-shaped, and still with evident grip, that might
not be lightly loosed.   Often has it seemed with
hands so gifted, as with eminent surgical operators,
as if there was a specialized individual life in them
quickened for their own wondrous operations.   Of
her almost incredible facility of handiwork her
after years gave ample proofs.   Once, in 1861, she
was left in her " work "-room (employment for
the soldiers' wives), and after a long morning in
the camp, on my return, asking how she had got on,
her quiet but staggering reply was that 40 shirts [a],
i.e. so many strong soldiers' shirts, had been cut
out by those spare, nervous hands alone !   It was
the same with more delicate work, women's spe-
cialities of household ornamentation, in wool or fret-
work ; and so with a great command of the most
difficult alphabets for church decorations, her power
of invention and rapid production were of rarest

[a] The exact words from my journal are, " ' An idle day.'
I have only cut out 40 shirts, 3 chemises, 4 dresses, sewn
on buttons to a good many things—O yes, and 4 night-gowns,
and other matters, &c."

quality. One festival-day, on which her handiwork
was more plenteous than usual, being Easter, with
texts and spring-flowers—chiefest the meek primrose
—one poor worshipper on entering the chapel
clasped her aged hands and fairly cried, "Why,
I thought I had jumped straight into Paradise!"
and she was not far away, could we but see behind
the veil of God's holy house.

Yes! that hand had wonderful power, despite of
her singularly small bones, which always made her
liable to sudden dislocations—the Ulna was "out"
at the wrist for many years. But the hand is a
universal and an immemorial study. All the world
over it has been felt to be such. It is a weird thing,
and a shadow of mystery is about it, which is really
the root of the old belief in Chiromancy! It is as
a sacrament of action, symbolic of good and evil;
a gift and a power. Outstretched and upraised it
is, in life, the sign of prayer or mute appeal; and
folded, on many a sculptured stone, it speaks for the
dead of their undying hope; and its almost *magic*
touch of sympathy (p. 89) is far beyond the measures
of science or cold philosophy. So the Psalmist ex-
pressed a very intensity of affection for the "city of
God," when he cried, "If I forget thee, O Jerusalem,
let my right *hand* forget her cunning." It may as-

tonish those who have not known or weighed the
fact, to learn how important and frequent is the ap-
pearance of the hand throughout Holy Scripture,
from the earliest times, in its manifold use, as sign
and symbol, instrument and "means of grace," from
Jacob's prophetic "laying on of hands" upon Joseph's
two sons, downward. From the most ancient of
days, it has no known *origin*, but it is an unconscious
interpretation of some secret of nature, and has attained the divine sanction for its use. So Moses
"laid his hands" upon Joshua as his successor, and
therefore Israel obeyed him. Onward, it was the sign
of the appointment and unction of kings, of the
consecration of the priesthood, of the conveyance of
all divine offices, and in the wide sphere of formal
"Blessing" in God's name. By it the individual
sacrifice was appropriated, and with it the mysterious
scapegoat was impressed. By it, in the New Testa-
ment, the sick were healed, the leper cleansed, the
deaf made to hear, the dead raised, and the grace
of Confirmation was bestowed by Apostles. So "the
right hand of fellowship" was St. Paul's adoption
into the Apostolic unity; and the betrothal in Holy
Matrimony is by the hand-pledge of unity. Yea,
even in secular things, the power of the hand is
confessed, where all solemn covenants and wills of

the dying are impressed with the mystery, used in
varying words, as testimony—"given under our
hands ;" "we have set to our *hands*," and "by our
hands and seals ;" and, in short, "what hath not
God wrought?" by "might of hand !"

Is that hand, then, that wrought so incessantly,
now still for ever? Is it become a "*dead* hand ?"—
that which had such special *life* for the work of God?
A high scientific authority declared once that he
"could *conceive* in matter the potency of all life,"
but that was an error of expression ; he might so
believe, but none can conceive it. *I* can neither conceive nor believe that that hand—in spiritual power
at least—is even now without its work before God,
doing, in some unconceived and inconceivable state
of being, the will of Him "whose hand and counsel
determined before" the earthly life of a soul and
its *after state*.

CHAPTER V.

——✠——

"Teach me, my God and King,
In all things Thee to see;
And what I do, in anything,
To do it unto Thee."—*Herbert.*

NE of the earliest of Miss Sellon's associates,
living in the same house before she took up
the sisterhood previously founded [a], " Miss Kate "
went not forth as a raw novice: bringing some years
of experience from union-house, cholera-ship, and
hospitals, and from straw-plaiting homes, she was led
on by providential circumstances to the front, when
chosen vessels were being called for, to be a standard-
bearer for dear England in the awful battle-field of
disease, wounds, privations, and suffering; and her
preparation was inwardly the deepest—a self-surrender
that knew no future care.   She kept her " Devonport
Breviary " (Sarum Use), but so large a book was,
to her practical sense, a little " out of place " on such
a mission, where each one was bounden " to lay

[a] Alas ! for founders, inventors, benefactors, whose fame and
reward are so often lost, the original donor and founder, whom
Miss Sellon succeeded, *died in neglect and poverty!*

aside every weight ;" and so it was left behind, but it is now before me. Her Devonport iron cross lies on her coffin.

The nurses were sent out under provision of a gentleman chosen by the Government, with forethought and ample supplies, so that there should be " nothing lacking " to the travellers' comfort; but let the story of the journey and the one great omission, in a religious undertaking, be told in an original letter, which may also undesignedly show some personal character :—

" British Embassy, Therapia,
January 12th.

" My dearest Marianna,—I cannot tell you how deeply delighted I was at receiving your letters; they are the only one oasis (and ever will be) in this dreary desert. But, to begin from the beginning: I left London on 2nd December at 5 in the morning, and reached Folkestone in due time, and crossed to Boulogne in a gale of wind. . . . . With a large amount of faith we allowed the fishwomen to take our thousand and one packages, and, strange to say, we all got our own. . . . . We remained in Paris till Monday. Our party was in number 51—fifteen of whom were Romish *Nuns.* I quite envied them;

from the moment we met at the station (where they came attended by their priests), sent out with the Church's blessing, to the moment of landing at Constantinople, their progress was quite an ovation : stop where we would, priests came to bless and strengthen. At Paris I *did* expect the clergyman from the English Embassy would have called to bid us 'God speed!' but no, the only blessing I received was from a Romish Priest, and when I bent my head to receive it I almost wept to think that it should have fallen from other lips. . . . . While at Paris I went to the services at *Notre Dame*, *St. Roch*, and the *Madeleine*. I cannot stay to describe any of these ; I will just say that not one was equal to an English *Cathedral*. We left on Monday and went to Lyons, where we passed the night ; it is 300 miles from Paris, and I never saw anything so miserable, so utterly devoid of beauty or interest, as the country between the two places ; we left next day, after I had seen the churches there, and went down the Rhone in a steamer. I was never more disappointed in my life ; I had heard of the beauty of the Rhine and the Rhone till my imagination pictured something exquisite : heigho ! heigho ! when I want to think of beauty I shall call up from the caverns of memory some sunny spot in blessed Eng-

land. We remained at Avignon next night, having
landed at Valence. The cathedral at the former
place is worth seeing. I went to the early service,
' while it was yet dark,' and then went on to Mar-
seilles, where we remained two days ; it is a nice
place, not equal to Lyons. My voyage (thence) was
something to remember. I was very ill, and the
weather was terrific : one night our skylights were
washed away and the sea broke over us, and of course
filled the deck and flooded the cabins, filling the
beds and deluging the occupants ; I never, never
shall forget the scene : the poor nuns, almost in
a state of nudity, called wildly to the men, who, in
like apparel, were wandering about, to come and
help them bale out the water from their beds ; others
calling on children, or on husbands ; some thinking
only of self, and all screaming most wildly, while the
water, up to our knees, carried everything before it,
fruit, railway-rugs, figs, oranges, stockings, basins,
in short everything moveable. The whole set, in
their terror, seemed to forget that the God who
holds the water in the hollow of His hand was as
near to them as when upon the Eastern waters He
arose and rebuked the wind and the sea, saying,
' Peace be still.' *I am no coward* [Editor's italics],
therefore I was able to look on and wonder, ready

to exclaim, 'O ye of little faith!' .... O Marianna, I could almost have spurned the whole created race. But to turn from this : the captain put into the port of *Navarino*, so, through the storm, we saw this *famous* place—a miserable village! We spent one day at Messina in Italy ; it is a glorious place. Oh ! the quaint old town, so like a picture ; we visited every church and convent there ; went to a nunnery and monastery ; *we* were not allowed to enter more than the church, where we stayed while the gentlemen explored the rest. I was sent forth with a blessing from one of the monks, owing, I suppose, to his taking me for a Romanist, because I knelt before the altar to examine some exquisite inlaid work. I cannot, therefore I will not attempt to, describe the beauty of the whole scene ; I would give a lifetime to pass such another day ; the intense blue of an Italian sky is beyond expression lovely. We spent another day at Athens ; this was the crowning glory of the voyage. I at last was in Greece, the place that had been to me the dreamland of life ; there stood the *Parthenon*, the *Temple of Jupiter*, and, above all, there was *Mars' Hill;* these things make Athens ; for all its beauty is won from the works of the mighty past. Just fancy one of the party, asking a French officer, when we came in sight of the

Parthenon, whether that was Athens, being answered,
' " Oh no, only (!!!!) some ruins five miles from it." '
What a soul the creature must have had, no bigger
than a mouse's ! I beg the latter's pardon for placing
it on a level with a thing that did not know chalk
from cheese. I must tell you all about Athens when
I come home ; language is too poor to express what
I felt. We stayed next day at Galipoli ; then at
Constantinople. To see this from the water, with its
domes and minarets gleaming in the exquisite sunlight, its groves of cypress-trees and its hanging
gardens, you would fancy it the entrance to Paradise ;
but go on shore ; try to walk there, and then say
what you think of this Eastern Lily ! there are no
footways; you and your horses are hail fellow *not*
well met, though you are obliged to keep all your
wits about you : if you go into a shop to buy a thing,
you give it to one man to carry home, and then
employ another to see that the first does not run
away ; then you must watch both yourself; the place
(and people) beggars description.

"We were obliged, instead of going to Scutari, to
come on to this place, Lord Stratford de Retcliffe's.
We have been tending the sailors at the hospital
here ; some nurses came to take this work yesterday
from England, so I go to Miss Nightingale to-morrow;

To face p. 35.

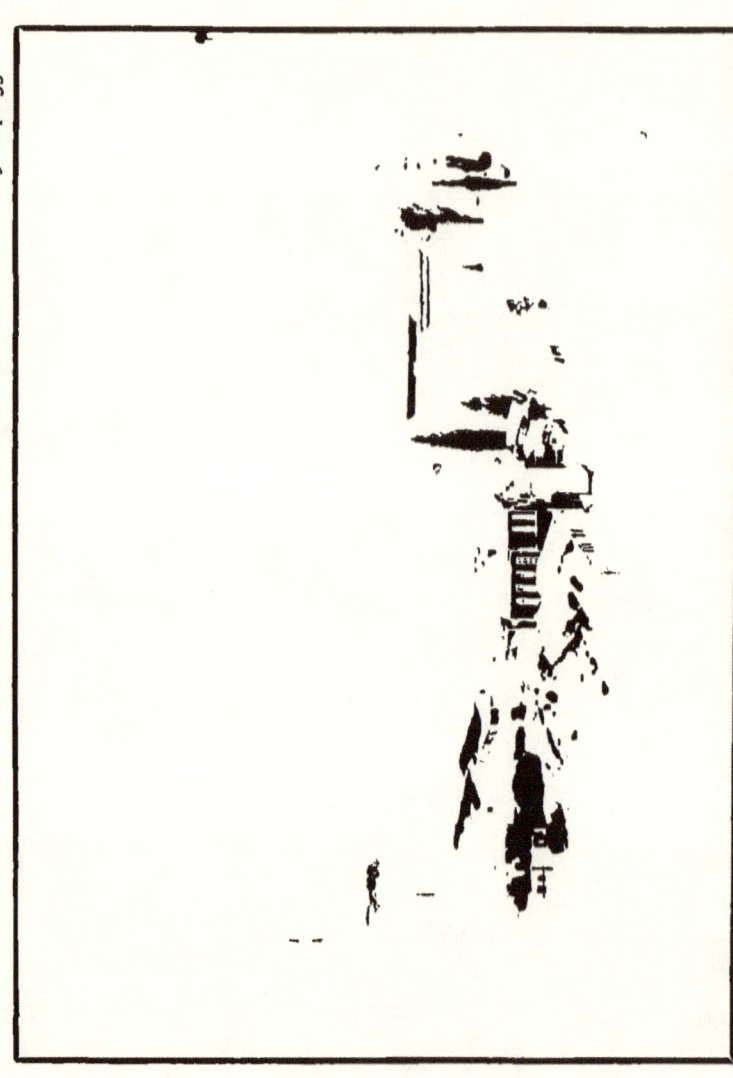

Scutari Hospital.—The Landing-place and Sea of Marmora.

From Editor's unfinished Pencil Sketch, 1855.

only a few of us are chosen to go there (Scutari), although there are there 7,000 wounded; the rest of our party go to a new hospital formed at Kululi. We have been here a month, and I have been house-keeper, and have been mentioned at the War Office as such. You would die with laughter to see the old nurses, when they come to my store-room, look at the *brandy bottles*, and, as if they were synonymous, complain how they suffer from 'them spasms.' Oh the luxury of providing for such a lot. I will not, dearest, promise to draw aside the veil that hides the misery of Scutari. God only knows the full, deep, dread horrors of the place. May He strengthen me for my work. Twenty-one times since I com-menced this have I been disturbed, therefore forgive errors, and do not measure my affection by my writing, but send to me when you can and dear Mr. L. Give my love to all; when I can write I will. God bless you both. Kiss all the children.

"Yours ever, KATE.

"The nurse whose letter appeared in the papers is sent home."

This letter is long, but it may help to model the statue I hope to present of a not ordinary soul. What a yearning it shows for a divine blessing! what a seeking for strength! what full-hearted pity and singleness of purpose—self-forgetting; and what solitariness of self-keeping! so loving and pitiful, and living to aid others; and yet there was in her always a calm reserve of life that might not be broken in upon—not least alone when most in a throng of work and society; always *forging on* secretly at the anvil of some purpose.

The following lines are interesting from their very simplicity; but there was in "Miss Kate" ever a vein of the child—simplicity, directness, and fervour, —with a truly masculine will and judgment :—

> " Father of mercy, look in love
>   Upon our little band ;
> We're leaving now our hearths, our homes,
>   Our blessed Fatherland.

> Father, we go in weakness forth,
>   Yet strong in heart and will ;
> Strengthen us more, that we may each,
>   Our mission-work fulfil.

> Father, be Thou our Guide and Stay,
>   Let now the Moslems see
> Whate'er the Christians do, oh God,
>   They do it unto Thee.

Father, bless those to whom we go,
  And teach them, mighty God,
To lift up contrite hearts as now
  They ' pass beneath the rod.'

Father, oh Father, one prayer more,
  Let from our full hearts come ;
May now Thy choicest blessings fall
  On the hallowed hearths of home.

Father, we leave our treasures safe,
  Beneath Thy sheltering care,
Whilst we go forth to do Thy will
  In earnestness and prayer."

Dec. 1*st*, '54.

CHAPTER VI.

——✠——

"There wounds and blood ; there wasted frames ; there loins
  Unloosed with life's outflow unstayed ; the rack
  And fever fire ; the shrieks and raving words ;
  The strong one's wrestling agony ; the tears
  And tender memories, always last to die,
  Of *mothers* far away ª . . . . ."

THE conditions of things on reaching the hospital at Kululi were, to ordinary Englishmen, simply unimaginable. It had to be put in *order* and *made* into a hospital first, and then, with the people to whom the managers must look for supplies of meat, bread, milk, and infinite occasional services—Turks, Armenians, Greeks, Jews, each with the " defect of his qualities,"—to keep the order in working trim was a task which needed nerves and weight of personal character. " Miss Kate " as housekeeper had the larger part of this organizing work, and on any deadlock occurring from without—cheating shopkeepers and dealers—she had to appeal to the great *Eltche* to " come down " upon the offenders. Once the meat for the patients was so unfit for food that

ª "Poor fellows, 'tis to their mothers they always turn at last."

she brought down the Great Man to the hospital;
but he had a horror of the place, and would not go
inside to inspect for himself; whereupon " Miss
Kate" seized a piece of meat, just received, and,
believing that things *subjecta fidelibus oculis* are
soonest realized, carried it upon a fork to the Am-
bassador, with the appeal, " Now, Lord Stratford,
would you *like* such for your breakfast ? " The wrath
of the dreaded one was manifest at the foul fraud,
and the little bit of womanly presumption (?) was
successful; but again there is nothing like a letter
or letters written on the spot, at the time, and in
the midst of difficulties, that can give a true and
vital picture of the realities of past days,—contemporary testimony is decisive.

" *Kululi*,
" *Feb.* 11*th,* 1855.

" THIS is the new hospital, and therefore *we have
all the misery* of Scutari, without *one* of its comforts.
We are indeed in a most wretched condition. We
have very small stores, and the fever is raging
most fearfully. I have two wards, and in one of
them 11 orderlies, and the serjeant, and surgeon are
dead. I am up in the wards from early morning
till late at night, and it is indeed most sad to hear

the wild ravings of delirium—the fever makes them
quite mad. We have had as many as nine dead
in a ward at once, and they are just sewed up in
a blanket, and placed uncoffined in a large hole.
This hospital is nearer the seat of war than Scutari,
so we get the worst cases now. Whatever spare
time I have I devote to writing letters for the men,
which is a great consolation to them. Many times
I send the letters, telling the friends at the end of
the death of him who dictated the beginning. I
buy milk for the men out of my own money, as
they long so for it, and it is not allowed them, and
I give as many shillings for what I could get in
England for as many pence. (I shall be quite ruined
if I continue it long, but while my money lasts they
shall have it.) The poor men are only allowed
certain rations, and the bread is sour and the meat
unfit to be eaten, even by people in good health.
Everything here is frightfully dear, but I must make
sure of what I want and purchase here, as there
seems to be a fatality attending all things destined
for the East ; they seem only to enrich the sea or
furnish the holds of ships. One box sent to me was
opened and the contents taken out. People here
quite ignore anything like *directions*. 'Tis a very
sad time, and it requires a strong, stout heart to

bear all, *still I would not for all the world be out
of it."* [Editor's italics.]

The previous extract, with others, was sent by the
recipient in England to Lady Canning (he having
seen her when some nurses were being started for the
East), and he writes: " Recollect that at this time
Lord Canning was a Cabinet Minister, and that
the Cabinet was then the object of the censure of
Mr. Roebuck's Committee in the House of Commons
and of. . . . Had I been influenced by a spirit hostile
to the Government I should have sent these extracts
from the terrible accounts of Miss Anderson, either
to Roebuck's Committee or to *The Times*, but as
I only desired that the truth should reach the proper
quarter *for a remedy*, I selected her Ladyship, who,
from all I had seen and heard of her, I considered
the most promising channel for procuring redress. S. S."

Lady Canning replied with " thanks for extracts
from Miss Anderson's letters, and. . . . regret to learn
that during her illness she was robbed of her clothing
by those who ought to have taken charge of her."
She also sent out an order for " her outfit to be made
up without loss of time," adding, " I have always
heard of the two Miss Andersons' exertions in the
highest terms of praise."

" The Hospital, Kululi.

" MY DEAREST MARIANNA.—I am sitting up in bed writing this. I really have not one spare moment: this is a new hospital, and Miss Stanley is the superintendent. She wished me to be with her, and I think it much better : she and Miss Anderson (Emily) and myself have *one room* between us ; we eat, sleep, and in fact do everything there. The fever is dreadful ; I was *three* days alone in my ward, I mean without a surgeon ; he had fever, and the serjeant and eleven orderlies ; those who assist me have been taken ; I am so surrounded by death that I have little time to think of the living. You must never think me unkind, dear, if I do not write. I wish you to look in the Clergy List and find a parish named Hocliff or Atcliff, I think the clergyman's name is Newman. When you find it just put the name on the enclosed letter and forward it ; it is to tell a mother her son's death ; he was quite raving ᵇ, so I could not be sure of the name. You can never fancy the state we live in, and I dare not attempt to describe it, for with *ten* letters to write *I shall see the sun rise before I sleep.* [Editor's

---

ᵇ Dean Stanley mentions this in " Memoirs of Edwin and Catharine Stanley " (pp. 340-1), and on my reading the passage to her, " Miss Kate " said, " For the first time I felt sick."

italics.] I have to write one letter to some school-children, charity-children, who have sent me some few shillings for the men. Poor little things, I must not neglect them. The poor soldiers are not allowed milk, and I buy it with my money, and shall while it lasts; 'tis all they seem to care for. We have Russians here, and this is the Turkish Barrack. . . . . Do write soon. I have had letters from all I shall in future call *friends*.

"Yours ever, my own dear Marianna, KATE."

I do not attempt to record the scenes and daily work in the *new* hospital, but these few letters serve to throw lightning flashes into the abyss of suffering and gloom, and also to throw up features of the *Character* of the writer. The following tells of her terrible illness, when the hirelings about her, sup-posing her as good as dead, robbed her of all her clothes and outfit, while she lay, without power to speak or move, though conscious all the time of the robbery. If ever action were heroic it was so here : nothing daunted the soul in that fragile body; no scenes of appalling anguish ; no physical suffering ; no heart-rending want; no rage of fever madness; no hopeless toil of ministry; no doctors' warning to de-part; no hazard of life; no overthrow by fell disease, with weary weeks of prostration, hovering between life and death !—all, and more than can be told, was seen and suffered in vain to crush the unconquerable will that, wholly given up to humanity's help, was beyond the power of anything earthly to move " or shake her trust in God." Truly a living author says of her, " I always feel her life was as truly given for others as if she had died in the Crimea, as she never was well again."

(TO THE SAME.)

"April 5th, 1855.

" . . . . I have been very, very ill, so ill that my life was despaired of. One of our Ladies is dead, and *all* the *others save myself gone home;* the Doctors told us all they would not answer for our lives if we remained : because we had had the fever *once* we must have it again. What a trustful set ! however, I shall stay and trust in God ; not one of even the paid nurses remains at Kululi; they seem to fancy the poor soldiers can live without help. I had malignant typhus, and though I suffered, oh ! fearfully, I am thankful that the lesson was given me ; *now I know all my poor patients suffer:* far from frightening me, it only makes me more devoted to my sad work, and

Catharine Leslie Hobson, 1855.

Convalescent from fever.

[Of this ' Hospital' photograph no other copy exists. The chemicals failed with time, and a slight rub blurred the face. 'Restoring' marred the features and destroyed the *expression*, and so, two attempts failing, it is given as here.]

if in the end I should find a grave in Turkey I am quite sure none of my true friends will think I gained it wrongfully. I cannot, will not, see my fellows die of want while I, by a little self-denial, can relieve them. [An earthquake is then named whilst 'Miss Kate' lay in the Hotel.] Miss E. Anderson was taken ill the same day I was, and we were sent to the entrance of the Black Sea (Hotel at Buykdere); she is a daughter of the late and sister of the present Sir C. Anderson, and knows your cousin, John Pearson; he restored her church at Lea. We are great friends; she and I shared the cabin on board ship, and she tended me when sick like a sister. Just fancy, dear, your notion and mine of Eastern luxury, burying ourselves in soft cushions of the divan! there is not a soft thing in Turkey: every pillow might, nay would, serve for a sledge-hammer, nearly all, even for beds, being stuffed with straw; when I was ill I was indebted to a naval doctor for a feather pillow. I have been over one of the Sultan's palaces, and there the things were just the same, most wretchedly uncomfortable. . . . . God bless you, dear Marianna, and believe me your affectionate "KATE."

Miss Emily Anderson went home in April and

saw the Queen, who sent a very kind message by her to " Miss Kate " during her illness.

On the Burial of a Lady Nurse.

"Listen ! now to the measured tread ;
See they bear *uncoffined* the dead
To yon long grave, that opens wide
Upon the sunny green hill side.

Listen ! once more, for 'tis heard again,
That rhythmic tramp of martial men ;
But now the *coffined* dead they bear
To one small grave made ready there.

Why is it, now, that one is laid
So fondly in a coffin's shade ?
And why, too, must the sleeper bide
Far from the others, severed wide ?

Why is it, too, that tears will fall
From eyes that seldom weep at all ?
Why is it, too, that women grace
The soldiers' lonely burial-place ?

It is that here, to-day, they bring
The grave a gentler offering :
No soldier hero now they bear,
'Tis woman claims their tender care.

She is the first of that small band
Who, from our dear own English land,
Came forth, in trembling hope and fear,
To work her woman's mission here.

Well may they weep, for they have given
One of their best-beloved to Heaven :
Well may they weep, for she is laid
Far from the Church's holy shade.

Yet while they weep the Apostate's sod
Is hallowed here by prayer to God,
And where, baptized, the dead are found
For ever must be holy ground.

And though no blessed church bells toll
A requiem for the parted soul,
Yet still her holy prayers are said,
Hallowing the graves of Christian dead.

Lay her then in her dreamless sleep,
In God's own acre still and deep ;
For guardian-angels now will be
Watching thy graves, sad Kululi."

"C. L. H." ("MISS KATE.")

CHAPTER VII.

——✠——

      *   *   *   *   *

"Be Thou our guide when joy gives birth
  To sunlight o'er the things of earth ;
  Oh let us not too closely cling,
  Father, to any human thing.

      *   *   *   *   *

"Father, if suffering there must be,
  Not, not on him, but oh ! on me
  Let it still fall . . . . ."
                       "MISS KATE," *Therapia, May,* 1855.

THERE were very frequent cases of "mistaken identity" in the reports sent to the English newspapers. As the best known figure among the lady-nurses, and in general charge of the work by government appointment, "Miss Nightingale" was to many a generic name to whom many things were assigned through mere ignorance and mistake. One picture appeared in an illustrated London paper, with the story that a soldier said to her, "Surely, Lady, you must be paid very highly, for you come to us at all times, *through the deep snow*, night and day." "Miss Kate" was the lady who was mistaken, and by her the soldier's remark was told to Miss Nightingale, whom she afterwards nursed. Her likeness was thought to be recognized in England by a friend who wrote to her mentioning the fact.

Again, Miss Nightingale is believed to have been the first to move about the nursing of the soldiers, but the truth is that Mrs. Mackenzie, the daughter of Dr. Chalmers, who worked at the sailors' hospital, Therapia, had started the idea. She actually wrote to Mr. Sidney Herbert proposing her scheme, and was answered that if anything could be done a lady well known to himself would be applied to. No one is to blame for such mistakes; the general or leader in such cases becomes a *representative* character, but to individualize noble action is no detraction from the merit of the chief figure, nor is it so intended here.

After the poor raving boy was taken, " Miss Kate " was not far off from the like suffering. In my turn of visits as chaplain from Scutari, going through the crowded and foul wards at Kululi, I saw the ladies at work, and there I first saw " Miss Kate," and was riveted by the sight of the gentle, fragile woman, not simply "smoothing the pillow," but, with an intent and calm earnestness, *supporting* the suffering soldier in her arms, and gazing upon each movement of pain with eyes that were as deep wells of pity and purity.

E

The fever came that was to be practically the end
of her Eastern work. After the long, long weeks of
suffering and delirium she became convalescent, and
I and another chaplain were then at Therapia, ill.
Near there, at the hotel at Buykdere, I found her,
then to me only a lady nurse "who was sick." She
was sitting alone in a large *salon* turned into a bed
and living room, and my visit was spiritual—to ar-
range for Holy Communion. Her face was pale and
statuesque in its deep repose; her hair had been cut
short, but two or three locks on her forehead were
recovering its former rich growth and colour slowly;
her smile, on her visitor's entrance, was as an eve of
peace, and *there* was that sheen of a nameless *look*
that riveted one, seeming to go behind and set you
in the foreground; and *there* also, when in converse,
was the strange mild power of her reflective eyes, as
of a spirit visible; thought and sweetness, pity and
tenderness, mingling into the deep rest of a far-off
land! Then, and in after days, I tried with pencil
or pen, unnumbered times, to show the peculiar life
and formal setting of her eyes, but everywhere, in
many a stray leaf or sketch-book, were attempts,
more or less finished, but all witnesses of failure or
wasted aim: I had tried the impossible; and only
my own soul might, unforgetting, preserve their

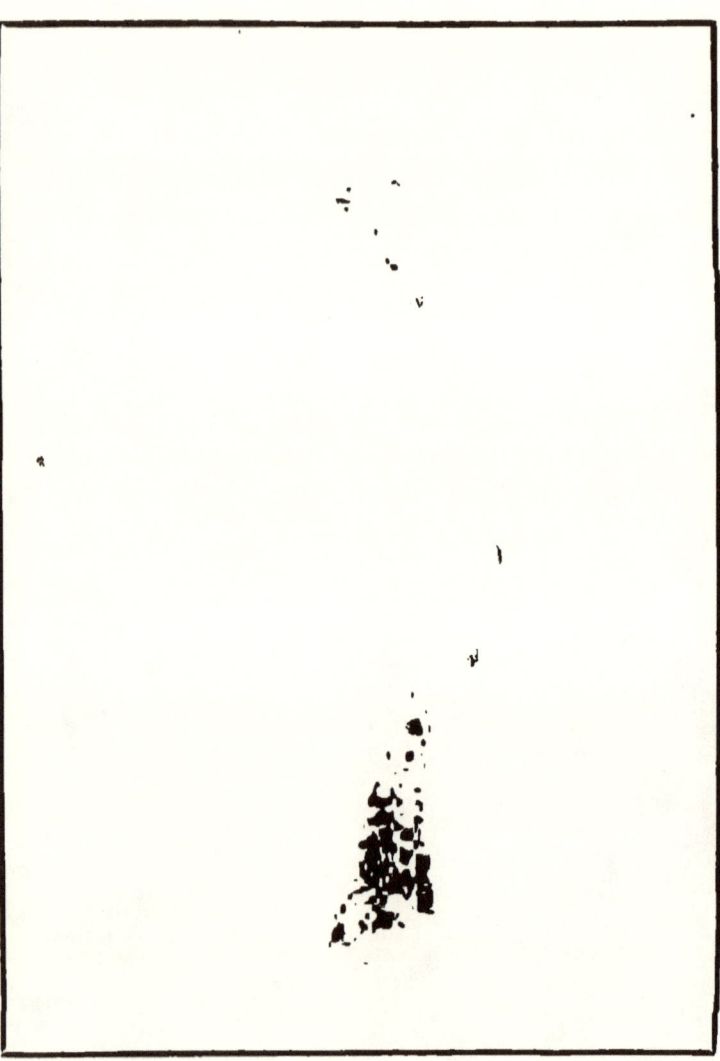

To face p. 51.

ASIA.

EUROPE.

Within a small radius here, are Therapia, Buykdere (Europe), and Kululi (Asia), on the shores of the Bosphorus.   *From Editor's Pencil Sketch.*

reality and wondrous grace, "a joy for ever" once—
now a memory undefaced. When she was able to
get about we walked and rode together in that lovely
scenery—sea and vale and wood and mountain—till
one day on the mountain-side, wandering for a view
of the Black Sea on the Asiatic shore, and looking
down upon the scene of her labours, *that* happened
which changed the surface of her beautiful personality, and made me the sharer of—and indebted to—
an "unbought grace of life," never sufficiently realized, alas! with all my admiration. She—I see that
far-off look of thoughtful calm even now—waited my
trembling speech and heard its end, and then the
Soul, so solitary in her inner life, softly bent her head
and murmured how great a thing it was "to yield
herself wholly into another's charge." The decision
was not lightly made, with which her work had no
slight concern—how that might be affected—but it
came with a gentle resting of her hand upon mine,
and a look of truth ineffable. There was peril to
her ideal of work, but her peril was my blessing,
and she really changed in nought, save the merely
outward phases of being; keeping ever her own individual life largely, apart but never alien to mine,
nor ever diminishing in pity and care, or ceasing to
keep the vision of poverty, ignorance, and suffering

before her, and "going forth to her work and to her labour until the evening " and the Master's call.

In a short time she was sent for a sea-voyage, and stayed awhile at Smyrna, feeling gradually her vocation to further work till the end, as we had contemplated, and beginning to go about with the most kind and attentive of doctors in the excellent hospital there; where the attraction of one of the seven churches, and the site of the martyr Polycarp's death and tomb, were very great, and woke up in after days many vivid memories; but the cessation of battles was near, and "Miss Kate" returned home on the proclamation of peace, with her hair still short, and a pallid face and wasted frame.

Fold back the page; its record is on high !

"Her judgment is with the Lord, and her reward with her God."

CHAPTER VIII.

——✠——

"Look here; upon this picture and on this."—*Shakespeare.*

"The whispers of thy gentle soul
   At silent lonely hours,
Like some sweet saint-bell's distant toll,
Come o'er the waters as they roll
Betwixt thy world and ours."—*Whytehead.*

FROM a ministry such as she had fulfilled, and from the fever-stroke that fell at last upon her, from the hourly horrors of battle, disease, confusion and death, for so long abounding, and as a memory unfading for ever, it was a release of unspeakable intensity to become again, on England's soil and in English homes, a loving visitant; "a watcher and an holy one," taught by ripened experience, and fitted for further ministries, to the suffering, the helpless, the neglected; and especially when her lot again fell amongst the soldiers, whose fellows she had so tended with unselfish devotion, even "nigh unto death." She was soon to give up her birth name, and take in holy wedlock another's,

but old friends, as before mentioned, still wrote to
" Miss Kate " for many years.   Many, alas! are the
ministers of religion whose office is reproached,
whose usefulness is hindered and whose life is made
a contradiction, through an alliance in Holy Matrimony with a woman whose worldly, wilful ways, un-
restrained by any true subjection to her husband's
ideal, and indifferent to the things that are to him
his life's obligation, ought to have forbidden him to
make such an one *his* wife; but, though there are
many, very many, good, irreproachable and useful
parson's wives, few, very few, have the responsibility
of winning and possessing, and becoming the guide
of a woman of singular qualities, of special fitness, of
a governing mind, independent, and of exceptional
knowledge of things parochial and ecclesiastical, and
whose whole soul was bent upon meekly using the
gifts she had for the welfare of those who have need.
Truly such a man "entertains an angel unawares,"
yet at his peril, and with an account to give of such
a treasure, at which I have again and again quailed,
and now confess with tender regrets and self-humil-
iation.

At the ancient church of P——, the scene of her
previous work, on returning after three years, she
found progressing the better order of services; and

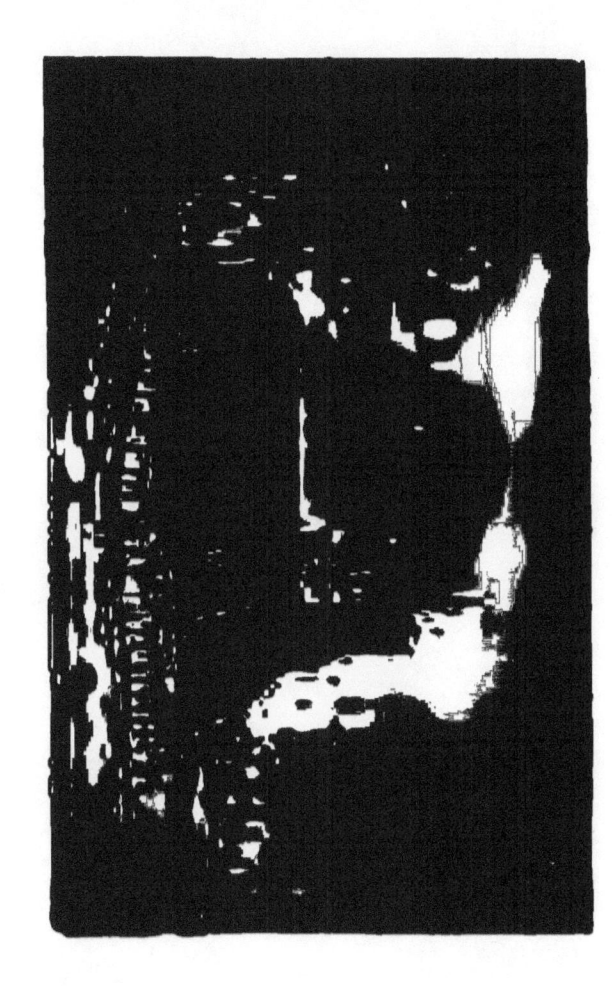

P—— Church, before Restoration.
From Editor's Pencil Sketch, 1856.

in the village were many to whom " Miss Anderson "
was as a name of reverence and loveable memory.
She went not to stay, but for a visit of two days, in
1856, and on the 2nd of August, on my sudden appointment to duty, she gave her life there at the altar
to be shared with mine; and " surely never lighted
on this earth " a woman more fitted to draw forth all
man's better soul and nature, and to sustain it by
an habitual reverence for her singular gifts and
graces, her lofty moral ideals, her power of will and
work, her strong judgment, her strange loveableness,
and her absolute unselfishness in act and thought.
A shadow of self is to most of us as inseparable as
the body's shadow; but with rare souls, at intervals,
this self-hood is thrown off, and, in her, it was dead,
" a despised broken idol." Always and unceasingly
her thoughts were, as by a second nature, going out
after and resting upon some design, action, or need
outside of self, and it was out of this side of her character that she grew early to care little for mere " ac-
complishments," though intensely sensible to every
reality in poetry, painting, music, or other gift—and
sometimes a scathing critic of any vital fault. She, in
short, was, beyond all else, devoted to the subjection
of everything to *use*, in the divinest sense of that
word—the best use of body, mind and spirit, and

to the "bringing of every thought into captivity to the obedience of Christ."

It is a strong example of her self-forgetfulness and respect for the high *use* of everything, and of rare strength of decision, albeit a vexing trial at the time to her concerned, that after the Crimean days—when her letters were regular and treasured—on an occasion of producing a bundle of these, her sister had to submit to her suddenly throwing them all into the fire, with the remark, "What is the *use* of keeping these after they have served their purpose?" Years after, another bundle of letters, after being "extracted" for a lecture, were burnt by misfortune, and the extracts are not to be found. From the specimens before quoted one may, without any prejudice of affection, think that to others, in after days, these memorial records would have been very precious, and of some hallowing *use* also, though she would not so think of any words of hers. Another example of this characteristic is that she preserved—or left behind her—very few letters from others, however near and dear ; one little old brown note from the clergyman whom she reverenced as an early teacher, at whose house she first became associated with Miss Sellon (the Rev. R. W. K——): two from " Henry, Exeter," and all my bits of verse to her, but no *bundle* of Epistles. Some special reason doubtless preserved these, though there is no record of such. The most of such relics are letters of the Bishop of Jamaica, in more recent years (1860—1872), and these are scattered about in books or other places. "How my dear father loved her," was not the only reason of the exceptional survival, but, with his facile and graceful pen, letters came often and again with some present of a book, or other gift, or with some verse—always "in the air," wafted on light-winged fancy—and his poet-daughter, Mrs. Harvey, dearly loved and loving, had the like reason for her letters being kept; who writes to me in my sorrow, "The thought of her is bound up in my memory as long as memory lasts; the loving, grateful sense of all her kindness rendered to me since the day I first saw her sweet face." "It was indeed a gracious love she gave me out of her generous heart—because I could so little repay her."

"After they have served their purpose." This was a widely operative word with her. It applied even to her wardrobe, and other mere personal belongings. She would wear some things for years, in despite of fashion-changes. Her dress, though simple, was rich in material—at least it was never poor—and yet it was kept up at an incredibly small outlay, com-

paratively with that of most of her friends.   Oil for
her hair cost nothing, for she never used it ; and yet
it was always glossy, as the well-groomed coat of a
thorough-bred.   The wild fancies of woman decora-
tors, reckless of the sacrifice of beauty and individual
suitableness, she never thought of following ; yet no
one would ever think of her as " out of fashion :"
fashion did not really seem to affect her, or be conspicuous by its absence.   She was never a " dowdy,"
or " old-fashioned ;" for as soon as her dress became
other than " fresh," it was discarded and given to the
needy or dependent, so that her changes came as
the flowers, in a settled order above the region of
caprice.   Goodness, beauty, and individual suitableness were her only rule.

CHAPTER IX.

——✛——

"Life is real, life is earnest."—*Longfellow*

" . . . . O God who lent me life
Lend me a heart replete with thankfulness."- -*Shakespeare.*

HER married life began at Parkhurst, and there
the soldier's habitual hardship was, as in every
place, if married and in excess of wives allowed to
each regiment, to find decent and accessible lodg-
ings at a price he could pay. She soon saw a way
of help. Quite near the barracks was a sort of
hamlet with its colony of soldier-lodgers, paying ex-
orbitant rent for a single room, and we found that
disputes had in past days arisen between the vicar
and the barrack chaplain, as elsewhere, about the
right of the latter to minister here. I soon proposed
to become the nominal curate of the place, so as to
act *for* the vicar, and we had no more difficulty.
Then, the Colonel commanding heartily concurred
in a plan for helping the well-conducted soldiers,
by our taking up certain cottages directly from the
landlord; partially furnishing them, and letting the
rooms at a lower rent than here, or in the town
of Newport, was usual. Such, of course, became

a prize, and were held out as an advantage to the well-conducted men.

Soon, in the next year (1857), the terrible Indian Mutiny fell like a thunderbolt upon the land, and at once the desolation of the wives to be left behind —with no pay or lodging—rose up in grievous sharpness, demanding relief. The wail of distress was loud—the recent Crimean war having shown the facts which were still fresh in mind. " Miss Kate " planned at once to get work for the forsaken women. I had a long letter inserted in *The Times*, explaining the little understood distress, and asking for help, in order to pay more than slopwork wages to the women, and to work up supplies of clothing for public sales.

This letter is before me now ; it had a sufficient response from far and near to enable us to anticipate the evil and be ready, as soon as the husbands were draughted away. The boon conferred was blessed, and it enabled " Miss Kate " to be sometimes " hard " upon careless and bad work, which—soon known to be sure of rejection—gradually disappeared. This scheme brought its organizer into immediate communication with the noble and generous founder of the " Central Association for Improving the Condition of the Wives and Families of Soldiers and Sailors," and later on of the " Patriotic Fund " (Major

Powys), which continued till his death; and many
were the poor children who were on her hands, and
were aided by him, in days long before any "honorary Secretary" was suspected of receiving from
such a charitable fund a secret salary! The good
Commandant was gladdened by the benefits conferred, and energetically worked the financial part,
whilst "Miss Kate" controlled the women's handiwork. Daily upon the hill where her workers were
lodged, it was here that she saved a little one, play-
ing upon the highway unconscious of danger, when,
quick as lightning, she saw a fierce bull close upon
the child, and at the risk, of course, of her own life,
snatched the innocent away from danger, when close
under the swoop of his horns. Truly she said before,
" I am no coward."

Her work at Parkhurst is sufficiently signified by
the following letter to me :—

"CENTRAL ASSOCIATION FOR IMPROVING THE CON-
    DITION OF THE WIVES AND FAMILIES OF
        SOLDIERS AND SAILORS.

"*Office, No. 7, Whitehall, S.W.*
"*Ap. 1st, 1859.*

"MY DEAR SIR,—Since I rec^d your letter of the
25th ult^{mo}, I have rec^d a letter from Col. Jeffreys, who

evidently shrinks from the greatness of the work proposed with reference to the work of the soldiers'
wives and families.   I laid your correspondence and
his letter before the Com[ttee] yesterday, and they also
hesitate in continuing this good work, so zealously
undertaken and carried out by M[rs]. Hobson and
yourself.   Much will depend upon your successor
as Chaplain, for I fear that unless he takes it up
warmly the work will fall to the ground.

" Colonel Jeffreys kindly offers to try the work for
three months, and the Committee in London are
quite ready to give any requisite assistance for that
time.   But should it not prove satisfactory to Colonel Jeffreys and the Local Committee, it had better
be abandoned, and the stock in hand sent to London, where a readier sale can be got for it.

" Very sincerely yours,

" H. L. Powys,

" *Major, Hony. Secy.*

" *The Rev. W. F. Hobson,*
    " *Parkhurst, Isle of Wight.*"

Her home here had the fairest outlook; from one
room, backward, the eye ranged inward and upward
over loveliest slopes and woods, to the centre of the
Island, and, in front, strayed away down the valley,

past Osborne, and out to the sea at Cowes; but on
our removal in 1859, the regret for the lovely spot
was soothed by the change to Shorncliffe camp.
There we hired a house on the cliff, with a hanging
garden going down to the beach, and looking out
on the wondrous highway of ships from all the world,
through the Straits of Dover. The ever-present sea
at your feet, and the white cliffs and lighthouses of
the French coast, were as a rapture of beauty and
enjoyment to the spirit, in her hours of work and
of refreshment, and never palled. Often straying on
the beach here, " Miss Kate's " eye once caught sight
of a piece of white cornelian, and further watchful-
ness brought her quite a harvest of pebbles, of various
kinds. One, cut into a cross, an agate, is four inches
in height.

There was at the camp the nucleus, or rather the
ruin, of a woman's hospital, supported by voluntary
aid, and of this " Miss Kate " becoming Lady Superintendent, she set up again its decayed places, and
got it into working order; when a purblind, captious
doctor set everything ajar, supporting a nurse against
the Lady Superintendent, till dismissed by higher
authority ; and finally making *voluntary* management
impossible. Subscriptions were withdrawn, and one
energetic supporter, Col. the Hon. G. D——, R.A.,

wholly withdrew his women from the hospital. " Miss Kate " also withdrew from the charge, and wooden officialism supplanted the tender humanities of private zeal. But this was only a side of her work, filling up the greater concern of helping and teaching the women of the whole camp. For this she brought with her the working scheme, and chiefly the shirt-work for hundreds of women. She had also touched the generous feelings of a northern cloth manufacturer, who henceforth, for many years, sold her bales of cloth at wholesale prices, so that she was enabled to sell to the soldiers' wives cloth for children's clothes at prices elsewhere unheard of. Her hands were full, and many came to help the good action by purchases and pecuniary help. County people, Brockmans, Deedes', came in constantly, and greatly sustained her. The idea was new, and was successful. Her public sales of the work carried off what private purchasers left.

With a keen eye for " situations " and a quick ear for " asides," there was not wanting many a choice anecdote of such, detailed afterwards to me with quiet but graphic point. It was not that she seemed to look or listen for such, but her intense sympathy, especially with the young, gave the unconscious power of catching everywhere the points of a scene

or a phrase with marvellous effect; thus, outside the
" Pavilion " Hotel, at Folkestone, she caught from a
small boy, with a butcher's tray on his shoulder, the
significant or saddening question to a companion,
" I say, Jim, what's you *sense* your han'sher with—
gin?" and, close at home, at a little by-path into
Sandgate, she heard, "I am going home with you
to-day," from one boy; and the reply, " Nay! not
to-day;" then, "O yes, I want to go to-day;" whereupon the situation became strained, but the other,
after a slight pause, answered in a doleful tone, " No
don't come to-day, for we have a *bad* dinner to-day,"
—not a bad hit—but with inimitable cunning and un-
answerable firmness the visitor settled the point by
a last word, " O yes, I *like* a *bad* dinner;" and he
went! The following is a mere incident, but friends
used to say that such things happened to *her* only.
A caller once appeared at the door, whom an old,
shy Kentish servant announced as " Elizabeth B——;"
but, her mistress having some visitors, she was bidden
to take the unknown " Elizabeth " into the kitchen
to wait; whereupon there burst into the room with
enormous laughter *Lady* Elizabeth B——!

The work continued here for four years, and the
first Government contract with a *private* manager
came, I believe, to *her* from Pimlico. The plan did

F

not at first work quite smoothly. Oftentimes shirts
were rejected for no visible reason, and in other cases
by mere routine blundering. Ultimately we got a
clear case ; a whole order for shirts was returned for
being made " *contrary to pattern ;*" whereupon I went
up to the Pimlico stores, and produced the condemned
shirts and the *sealed* pattern to the officer in charge
(Col. D'A——), and lo ! the pattern sent to us had
been superseded ! A fault of this kind, and on a
large scale, was the least likely to be found in her
work, for method, exactness, and practical knowledge of the *meaning* of any change of pattern were
things of daily use.

One of the most painful cases I ever experienced
occurred at Shorncliffe. My soldier-orderly's daughter disappeared suddenly, and was lost for some
weeks, in spite of police and every kind of search.
At last she was found in an officer's hut, dressed in
men's clothes ! It was a most tickle case for me
to move in, and ominous warnings were not wanting, as being a non-official concern to me, but *only*
" moral " (!), and I might " get into trouble," &c.
However, I sent for the officer's father (a General),
and, with the girl's father, and supported by the
colonel of the regiment, in my own house enforced,
with a written agreement, a provision for the ruined

child, in some "refuge" or "home." But the poor father was so enraged, and was of so violent a temper —beating her till the mother was afraid of his killing her—that "Miss Kate" brought her away, with the mother's help, to her own home and kept her for three weeks, whilst ill and her condition doubtful, and *personally* "took care of her" till she was able to be sent away.

For this unworldly-wise interference, and to force the money put into my *trust* into the father's own disposition, we suffered every available annoyance, and finally (despite of my warning) a law proceeding, which consumed most of what should have benefitted the poor girl, in expenses, and burthened the father with debt. It was the fate of those who interfere between man and wife, both against the outsider! but it was, none the less, action for which the colonel and officers were grateful.

CHAPTER X.

—✠—

"Man dressed in little brief authority."—*Shakespeare.*

". . . . thousands at his bidding speed,
And post o'er land and ocean without rest :
They also serve who only stand and wait."—*Milton.*

ROM Shorncliffe we went abroad for some months, on an invalid tour, moving about from one quaint old German town to another; with many a sketch and frequent verse; from Aix-la-Chapelle, the historic home of Charles the Great—

"Aquisgranum Urbs regalis,
Sedes regni principalis "—

and the dream-land of ecclesiastical legend—

"Where piety seems to walk by sight,
And faith is an earthly substance bright :
Where reason maunders to prove each show,
And lowly faith to doubt is slow "—

we made for the Danube. Omitting the well-known charm of Cologne's then unfinished Cathedral, and those of Coblenz and red Mayence, we left the Rhine at the latter place, and reached old-world *Bamberg*, dear to memory for its repose and picturesque beauty of surroundings; its solemn and soothing Cathedral, with the few women and children at private prayer, in pews; and such ancient costumes! *Nuremberg* came next, with its not beautiful Cathedral, where, inside, the *Protestant* service, scant and gloomy, made one feel a most uncomfortable sense of disproportion between the large interior and its now comparatively mean uses; nor was it easy to forget the strange pictures still allowed to hang on its Protestant walls; one of which might well be covered with a veil. Very rich in interest is the old once "free" city; famous for its industries and its artists—Dürer, Vischer, Kraft, and Stross—in sculpture, wood-carving, metalwork, and a variety of inventions. From Nuremberg we sought the fossil caves of Bavarian "Switzerland," where masses of extinct creatures have left their bones to be encrusted with the thick stalagmite, under roofs of stalactite, alike the drippings of the limestone rock through untold ages. Along one valley of this formation, from Muggendorf, the crags on either side are often perpendicular, and look like sculptured forms; here we called aloud, "see there that old Viking," and sketched him; and there a Virgin Saint, with lamp in hand, stood out against the horizon at a sharp turn of the road, perfect; and *she* was booked at once also. A little anticipating, I here mention Münich,

though in our route it came after Regensburg.   What
a Cathedral ! externally the ugliest brick erection ;
with really no interior charm to redeem it ; whilst
the realistic picture of the Blessed Virgin, with a
huge cloak sheltering " all estates and conditions of
men," is trying for its inscription—

> " O tu quæ sola potens æterni numinis iram
> Flectere; tege nos virgineo diva sinu ; "—

but the City itself charmed, with many attractions
of art, and with Churches, specially the Chapel Royal,
a gem of beauty; with sacred scenes, painted by
chief artists, adorning the walls throughout—com-
parable for charm only to Pugin's rich and beautiful
Chapel at Hale's Place, Canterbury—too little known
heretofore by lovers of high aim and finished work
of price—now in the hands of Jesuit Fathers.   The
bright waters of the—

> " Isar rolling rapidly "

complete the feeling of freshening life gained by the
visitant to Bavaria's capital. From the old free
city of Nuremberg we went to *Regensburg* (the city
of seventeen sieges), also " free " of old, and famous
beyond comparison with its present condition.   It
has a " street of ambassadors," showing its olden
stateliness, when the high road of traffic went through

it, and by the Danube to the East. In Church
History it is conspicuous as the scene of many
Councils, under its early name, Ratisbon. Its glorious Cathedral—succeeding two others in ruins—is
unique for beauty and features peculiar to itself.
The rich western front with its twin spires, like
St. Ouen and Salisbury, has a sculptured, triangular,
and projecting porch—allowing of two doors outside
the great inside one. Within, on either side of the
latter, are two circular niches, each holding a medallion head; the one a sweet old woman's face, called
"the Devil's grandmother;" a ·puzzle I can only
guess at from Milton's words—

> ".... His form had not yet lost
> All her original brightness ....."

as suggesting his pristine purity and goodness.
In the nave, by the south door, is a draw-well, sculptured, and presenting two life-size figures of our Lord
and the Woman of Samaria. The rare and soaring
sacramental *hauslein* is in a sort of retreat, behind
the high altar; but to ordinary visitors the most
curious peculiarity is the singular—I believe *solitary*
—echo at a particular spot in the nave, which the
sacrist awakes by a musical note with the voice,
and which goes upward with magical effect, floating,
as it seems, spirally, higher and higher, to play

amongst the highest reaches of the interior roof, until it gradually dies away. The old bridge over the Danube, and its boy figure, gazing with shaded eyes upon the Cathedral spire, rivets one by its still naturalness.

O what calm and rest these relic cities of days by-gone offer to the tired and sickened struggler in this nineteenth century's wild haste, and reckless, consuming rush !

There, were written the following "Lines on the banks of the Danube," simple, but showing my subject's life ideal, and adding to her portrait :—

"Blessed river, ever flowing
    To thy home, the far-off sea;
Bringing, in thy rushing gladness,
    Many visions unto me.

I sit idly by Life's river,
    Noting not how swift to run,
Into Death's great shoreless ocean,
    While life's work is still undone.

I have only cared for duties
    That seemed tempting, grand, and high :
Closed my heart against the whispering
    Of the many, nestled nigh.

Oh, my Father, make me listen
    Humbly to these voices sweet,
*Till I bring my finished mission
    Safe to my Redeemer's feet.*"

By this time the shirt-making for Government was so established, that my successor in 1862 could take it up without difficulty, and it has ever since been at most military stations the greatest boon to the soldier, in securing him the best possible shirts at less than contractors' prices; but it is not generally known that the idea arose as I have mentioned and that the Indian Mutiny was its earliest date, and "Miss Kate" its originator.

I only recall one or two illustrations at P——Dock, our next lovely home, Whitehall, and on Milford Haven, where "Miss Kate" was concerned. Two "Irish Protestant" Clergymen were the only Church of England Clergy there. Each abused the other to me vilely, till I refused to hear either. Having no chapel for the troops, I had obtained permission to use the Dockyard Chapel, at an hour before one of the above used it as naval chaplain. He was thought to be *spirituous* in the pulpit, whilst the other, as Parish Clergyman, was so utterly despised, that "liar" was the commonest epithet applied to him. Thus was the Church of England represented, whilst the dissenters had *six times* the number of her services. The land was indeed *barren and dry!* Soon, my early service, from this cause, was attended by the Dockyard officers, living in the yard, and by the townspeople; whereupon the two Protestants, as Herod and Pontius Pilate, were "made friends" to oppose me; and, finally, the Superintendant of the Dockyard was so wrought upon, that he issued an order forbidding naval officers to attend the early service, and set a policeman at the yard door to prevent the entrance of townspeople, unless military, or "officers' wives." The Sunday following "Miss Kate" found the policeman at the gate, and being demanded if she were an "officer's lady," she calmly but sternly said "No!" and steadily walked on without stopping; leaving the poor policeman dumfounded, and wondering at his despised authority! Before the next Sunday's service, I had presented the outrage at the War Office, with such *lights* upon the real circumstances, and with such life and death protests, that the Superintendant Captain had to instantly *cancel his own order!* Our stay here was short—though full of incident as to my duties—on account of the purposed removal of the troops suddenly; afterwards given up, on the Welsh Member's opposition in parliament.

The other touch, from the same place, for my portrait sketch is amusing. We had a lady friend of the family, who was short-sighted, and very unstable as to her "poor feet," who, moreover, was not then

a practical person at all; clever, with *perfect* board-
ing-school instruction and knowledge, and withal
a questioner of doubts and things "beyond the
reaches of our senses." She, walking with "Miss
Kate" on the wretched pavement of the place, de-
faced with frequent holes and often full of water,
suddenly appeared seated in one of these watery
traps, with feet uppermost, and with vexed exclamations, crying, "*How* ever did I get here?" *but not
moving out of her pit*, till "Miss Kate," sharply as
her suppressed sense of the ludicrous permitted,
retorted the *practical* question, "But *why* don't you
get up you ...?"

At a few days' notice, with a large house on hand,
I was sent to "the most important station in England" (so the then C. G.'s letter said); a few days'
respite refused, because "there would be no service
on the following Sunday" if I failed. I arrived on
Saturday night, and found that I was not wanted,
and the services provided for! Such play-things
does officialism, with some men in "brief authority,"
make of its subjects. On "Miss Kate's" arrival
her new home was not available for some weeks,
and we had to be cramped up in a small lodging
till a favourite chaplain of the C. G. found it con-
venient to move. It was a note of our first atten-

dance at the church services that this chaplain's wife was unable to repeat the word "Catholic" in the Creed, for which she substituted "Universal," avoiding the force of the synonym, as she thought, by a private non-natural interpretation. She was a Swiss Protestant, and the two retiring chaplains (brothers) were Irish Protestants. My mission was to satisfy a better feeling that had reached the place, and to organize a different order of services. The work was hard from the first, with a General Commandant, who marched into church with his sword uplifted, and did not know as to what his proper authority in things pertaining to divine services was restricted. An anecdote told later on shows "what manner of man" we had to deal with. As soon as we had possession of our house it was furnished afresh, and quickly put in order, and even at W——— was found beauty. My "Senior Chaplain's" quarters looked out far away over the common, with its wayside trees, even unto the mighty modern Babylon, and very rich were the sunsets through the magic mist and vapour over the long flat tract of intervening vicinage; the peculiar atmosphere throwing off those strange effects which Turner used to study with such artistic joy.

CHAPTER XI.

——✠——

" Making truth lovely, and her future might,
Magnetic o'er the fixed untrembling heart."—*Coleridge.*

N the fresh scene there were many strange arrangements to be met, the place having for years been wholly in the hands of extreme Evangelical and Presbyterian teachers and people. Very shortly "Miss Kate" came upon a "Mission woman" in her barrack visitations, and found her very sweet, too sentimental, blundering and impractical ; and such an one she simply *declined to support,* leaving her in the hands of the managers in which we found her ; but this was rashly set down to " Miss Kate's " High Church views ; until, at a not distant date, her own clique had to discharge her. Then, this agency and a women's hospital were worked by voluntary support, but there was one presiding " superior person," the General's wife, whose *official* philanthropy was very hard to work with, and to proportion to the deeper reality of another. This lady was the faintest figure in human solid flesh that could be imagined. Once very pretty, and still with a face of uncommon piquancy, yet with the stamp of fragility

so evident, that to "fade away" like a picture or
a dream seemed natural to her. Any proper *work*
was not to be looked for from her; yet, supreme and
dictatorial she would be, in despite of the lack of
use and experience. The other chief actor was a
woman of simple, direct, practical understanding (now
Lady L.), with intimate, personal, and *sympathetic*
knowledge of the ways and wants of the soldiers
and their wives. The amateur, official "Lady Boun-
tiful," and the stedfast, practical benefactor and
manager were generally in a crisis of strained re-
lations, on points of management or more general
aim. On which side "Miss Kate" would naturally
be found, her life and experience—the steady, still,
inflexible seeker of the best *end*, for a work's sake
only—there could be little doubt. She, as a mere
point of judgment, coincided with the wiser head,
yet she took no action at all, but simply kept to
her other work all the more. Alas! neutrality or im-
partiality was not to be tolerated by official arbitrari-
ness; and, moreover, the women's difficulty might
be a handle for a malevolent feeling in certain Church
matters; and so a General Officer and Commandant
did not think it beneath him to carry up to the
War Office his wife's complaint; and lo! I was sent
for, and met the Under Secretary of State and Lord

W. P—— professedly to reply to some charge against *myself;* but the first thing done was the putting into my hands a letter left by the General. On looking at which I instantly folded it up and returned it to the Under Secretary, Sir E. L——, saying, "This is a woman's letter, on women's matters; I positively decline to notice it; but I am ready and anxious to 'answer for myself' on any point;" and, turning to Lord W. P——, an old bachelor, I asked, "Would you have anything to do with women's matters, Lord William?" To which the reply, with a twinkle of the eye, was, "Not if I knew it." My answers on other petty points were satisfactory, and then I said, "Now, Sir Edward, I will if you please take the woman's letter, and get a woman's answer from Mrs. L." The letter was handed to me at once, with the remark, "Ah! she is a very old friend of mine." No more was heard of *that* letter, and "Miss Kate's" pity was apportioned between the woman who had caused, and the General Officer who had stooped to such action, but she was no further moved; she—

"‎.. heeded not, her heart was far away."—*Byron.*

In a very short time there gathered about "Miss Kate" a mass of work, and some 300 women were

taken up by degrees for employment. Commanding
Officers were glad for their poor women's sakes.
Things were stirred in their hoary and mouldy
routine, and the officials at the Army Stores (where
women—bad and good from any quarter—were with
loud scandal promiscuously employed at slop wages
for shirt-making) were greatly startled when orders
came from the War Office to open out to " Miss
Kate" all the material on hand, and to give every
aid to her enquiries. The issue was that enormous
stock, not known or on present record, was found,
and very soon the responsible War Office official
(G—— R——) gave " the control of the work and
the employés into ' Miss Kate's' hands," and, as
with Joseph, " whatsoever was done . . . she did it."
The *morale* of the women was looked into, and the
scandal of improper characters removed ; the wages
for work were raised, checked by the rejection of
any bad work, and an enormous profit was displayed
—theretofore the contractor's cruel gains. Soon
" Miss Kate" got from her old friend, Miss Stanley
—then become a member of the Church of Rome—
a *market* for the shirts, through her Westminster
Depôt[a]. A room was granted in barracks for giving

[a] Miss Stanley is another "catch" for "H. J. Coleridge,"
Jesuit, who, as with Lady G. Fullerton (p. 11), is made to

out and receiving shirts, and a regular service of transport began between W—— and Westminster, which went on through a superior serjeant " told off " for the service, who had charge to put the shirts into the carriers' hands (Parcels' Delivery Company), and did so ; but, alas ! the Westminster management was defective, and proper receipts for deliveries of goods were often delayed, and even altogether omitted, till " Miss Kate," anxious for her trust, and finding the carrier refused *receipts* for goods, ap-

appear as a Roman Catholic convert from *conviction*, through reason and logical acceptance of the claims of that branch of the Church, but in both cases without an atom of solid proof. Their cases were variants, but meeting notably in one point — their lack of the true spiritual *life* of the English Church, and of anything more than a mere superficial conformity to her *order*, unsustained by any firm grasp of her *historical position*, or a practical knowledge of her *teaching*. Such conditions of "religion" are a ready preparation for the attractions and influence cunningly brought to bear upon some. With no strength of conviction or of knowledge, they become easy captives, *outside* the sphere of reason or logic, and illustrate the LORD's word, " He that hath not, from him shall be taken away that he hath." In the case of Lady G. Fullerton, I am able to sustain my view by her own declaration to an earliest and dearest friend ; and, as to Miss Stanley, by her own solemn account to " Miss Kate." To suggest that the latter was, beyond her brother, the Dean, of "a *manly* courage and a firm and *logical* mind," is an amusing bit of imaginary knowledge and gossamer artifice.

G

peared at the depôt, where at once the mischief was discovered: but, alas! the past was irretrievable. Police and military pressure, detectives and the company's exertions—promised to me at least—all failed to find out the guilty. At both ends of the service there must have been thieves, whose cunning succeeded so far as to cause a loss of some £120 on the shirt account! "Miss Kate" was calm, but deeply moved—as evil always wrought in her—and I was in wrathful anxiety, till one morning a noble fellow, commanding the Horse Artillery, came to my barrack office, being a strenuous approver and supporter of the work for his women's sakes, and bluntly asked, "Now who is to bear all this loss?" to which I responded, "Myself." Quick as thought the tall figure sprang from his seat, and, his flashing dark eyes fixed upon me, with beauty in his words beyond elegance, he cried, "I'll be hanged if you shall!" A cheque-book settled my trouble at once, and the money was made up by my benefactor's efforts with his brother officers. Good, simple, heart! he was puzzled, and asked honestly, "What are my women to do if Mrs. Hobson gives up her work?"

Alas! in no long time "Miss Kate" had to submit to a severance from her thriving shirt business, and

from other work, on Church grounds not affecting
her ; but the story and its last episode may add
a stroke or two to my statue; and here is another.
In our early action (she as the mission-woman's con-
troller (p. 77), and I as chaplain, supposed to be
in a measure responsible for her and the Scripture-
readers), Colonel Gordon, the brother of the true
martyr Charles, a Presbyterian, but thoroughly religious, looked at us, myself especially, as actuated
by " High Church " feeling in respect to the mission-
woman, and so was sometimes *very* wroth, and supported her generously and passionately, till, bit by
bit, the wall of his prejudice crumbled, and the light
got through the chinks here and there as to his
protégé's unfitness.   Then, more intercourse warmed
two spiritual men to concord, when *High Church*
views were seen to be not against the higher spiritual
life, and at last, with noble impulse and unusual
self-restraint, above the clique of the dominant party,
he came to me and said, " Well, Mr. Hobson, I can't
agree with your Church views, but henceforth *I will
never again oppose you !*" Of course " Miss Kate "
was included in the word, and her quiet powers of
work and insight are brought into relief.   Opposition
died in the presence of real work and a candid
spirit.

Truly there is "Low Church" and "Low Church," "Evangelical" and "Evangelical." In every name, alas! men come to be zealous for the name and forget the power that made it honourable; they feed upon the husk, and discard the fruit of the inner life, and "leanness withal" is in their souls! The two Gordons I have known, of one family, the "martyr" and the above, have both been singularly real, and sympathetic and candid; and hence, with dissentient beliefs, an extreme Presbyterian Protestant took the High Churchman for "faithful," and walked with him in loyal peace. So, another brother clergyman, once, under a foul persecution, showed a like noble temper. He was of the early Evangelical School of Venn and Simeon, but, brought to my chapel on resigning his vicarage of thirty years, he, *unknown to me,* wrote to the Archbishop of Canterbury (Tait) in refutation of an evil charge against me—

"*Faversham, July* 3, 1874.

"My Lord,—During the eighteen months that I have been resident here close to the Alms-House Chapel . . . .

"I can bear my testimony to his preaching *a full Gospel, in the most simple manner, so that all that will may understand.*

"Richard Mosley."

The writer sent me a copy of his letter at once, with a note, as follows :—

"DEAR MR. HOBSON,—I have said what I thought your ministry deserved. May the Lord bless it.

"But I wish I could say that you never turned your back to the people, nor put up a cross in your chapel, &c. Yet I know these are very inferior things, in my mind not worth a thought compared with preaching the Gospel, therefore I have acted as I have, *on my bended knees.*

"RICHARD MOSLEY."

My instant reply was, "Your letters make up for another persecution," and I still think the above worth preserving, as an example for nominal *Evangelicals.*

With all the labour of the shirt-work cutting-out, distributing, examining each thing before it was paid for, and much correspondence, "Miss Kate" was her own book-keeper. She knew nothing of single or double entry, and her system was not known to science, and was not in *man's* way; yet she never was in confusion, never failed to make tally the debtor and creditor sides; and for years afterwards, in her sales for the Kilburn Orphanage ("Sisters of the Church") more than £2,000 were thus guarded.

Not the smallest sum—apart from small receipts at
public sales—was unrecorded, not a name or " sale "
was omitted.   Parsons and women are proverbially
bad accountants, but " Miss Kate" had an instinct,
in her own way, for exactness, and withal, her friends
said she had *a fairy army to help her!*

CHAPTER XII.

———✠———

" An emanation seems to go from him."—Tyndall.

ONE more touch at my growing statue is brought to mind by recent letters—the power of attraction and influence over others. What and whence is that potent mysterious power, "influence?" It is not always describable: it is only known by its effects; it does not depend upon mere intellect, knowledge, talent, or even genius. Strength and power, or wealth or station or liberal bountifulness, all may fail: it is an inherent, personal gift. It is ultimately, no doubt, *character*, yet not always definable in one word, "as one should say" of its possessor, "he or she is" so and so—"so able" or "so good"—albeit certain qualities are ever admired in whomsoever found; but "influence" is very often not "proportionable," for it is often said of one or another "he is this or that," or "he is so good and clever, and yet he has so little influence!" Men are strangely won by woman's purity, courage, truth. Women by self-forgetful sympathy and a lov-

ing tranquil *aloofness* from *their* common aims; and
so "Miss Kate" attracted both amazingly, and influenced them.   One writes that she was "so much
above the type of ordinary women;" and the wonderful way in which "confidences" were habitually
sought and given by aching and doubtful hearts was
a sure testimony to this unsought power.   Hence,
in no small degree, came her wondrous penetration
into character and facts.   None ever seemed able to
harden themselves—as so many find the guilty do—
against that pure, pitying, loving, penetrating gaze.
Once I remember a case of immorality and scandal,
and the woman persisted in her innocence, and
resisted every appeal for a confession; and her mistress complained to "Miss Kate" of her *wicked*
resistance and *defiance* of advice under grievous ac-
cusations.   *She* had accused, besought her to confess,
quoted Scripture, made solemn appeals, and worried
her with secular "preaching and preaching" against
such *sin,* but with no effect, save to steel the culprit
against yielding.   In short, "all that could be done,"
the mistress said, "had been done," and yet she was
unmoved.   One thing only was lacking—that "*touch*
of nature which makes the whole world kin."   Condemnation, not sympathy; denunciation, not "the
still small voice" of pity, had alone been tried.

"Miss Kate" saw the hardened woman, and a few tender tones only were heard, with an eye looking sorrowful and pitiful, when, laying her hand gently upon the culprit's arm, she said, "You *are* guilty," whereupon the sinner brake down and confessed, weeping her evil way and laying her abashed head upon that *sister's* breast in sure trust. It may seem a light matter to notice, or with no real connection with her past life, but it is singular that, before the end, her own devotion to the soldier was repaid in kind by a soldier-servant, who was engaged little over a year with his true "nurse" of a wife. The devotion of each was peculiar, but his was of the strangest type. He had learned from his wife, and been witness, of his mistress's private suffering ; and always, on preparing the table for meals, first asked shyly after her state. When her short rallying time, in St. Luke's summer, came, he drew her about in the Bath-chair—gently and watchfully—for she could not endure vibration or jolting ; and many brief moments of converse thus occurred—with all her power of *drawing out* confidences unsought — so that when the visiting-angel came in her last prostration, "Thomas" had become deeply attached to his mistress ; and tenderly did he help in the weary morning journey downstairs and back again at night.

Then, when confined to her room, he for a while did not see her. He had, moreover, a strong shrinking from the sick chamber; from seeing suffering and from death; but his honest devotion overcame all, and he would watch and wait, in the passages outside the room, in order to help; trembling, as he told his wife, when the sufferer became so thin that every movement was with pain and anxiety, yet always ready and prepared, as he declared, to " do anything in the world for my poor mistress," who came at last to *choose* and depend upon his help above all; and whose fainting breath and almost inaudible voice murmured "Thomas" day and night, in her need, with her pleading, grateful look. When the end at last came the faithful soldier wept, yea sobbed, like a child, moving about the house with hushed footfall and in silence, save the frequent moan of " O! my poor, dear mistress." His service was still needed for the one that was left, and, whilst lying on his chair-bed in the kitchen, waiting, the tears would stream over his pillow, and in his sleep his dreams were still, with weeping, of her whose sufferings he had so helped to soothe!

" Miss Kate's " power over *young* womanhood was special. In their griefs and disappointments; in their " beating against the bars " of thwarted hopes, they came to her, feeling, in some mysterious way, that she would be helpful, or at least share their misery with loving wisdom; but not only *young* hearts felt thus : A shrewder, stronger mind than that of an " elder lady" who wrote thus to me is rare; " It has not been my privilege to know another like your dear one. I was very fond of her. She was the only one I could open my heart to, in the anxieties and sorrows of those days. She always had comfort and holy thoughts to help me with :" and two younger women, now true wives of good men, once artillery officers, say severally, " I always look back to your time at —— as the beginning of any parish-work E—— and I ever did; and I hope it taught me to think and care for the well-being of others." " If ever there was a true, dear, good woman upon earth it was dear Mrs. Hobson. It was she who first taught A—— (the previous writer) and I to be helpful to others." Other "like words" are to the same point from those elsewhere, who lovingly remember the past days of her influence. Wherever she had a work she was found with a circle of young hearts and hands around her as helpers ; drawn, *not* by the work she gave them to do, but drawn by her to the work ; and her sway was alike with the well-born and the lowly. It was so at Shorncliffe; helpers were drawn to the work, as at Parkhurst, and more than even in the much larger action at W——. What a gift this power of attraction and influence over others' lives is ! No one may fully measure it now ; the touch of this power, once felt, is borne afar, to reproduce through future years and various fields the good seed of noble purpose and dutiful action ; and thus to draw out one human soul from the withering blight of selfishness, and to be the means of implanting a higher sense of life's purpose, is the attribute only of a few original and essentially *ruling* natures. " Miss Kate " was a ruler born, but not by the strong arm, or this world's means : it was solely by a genius of insight and pure intention—" charity out of a pure heart " that " never faileth."

CHAPTER XIII.

———✠———

"The nameless unremembered acts of kindness and of love."
Wordsworth.
" Now I am here what wilt thou do with me?"
G. Herbert.

AFTER another change of scene, a repeated
illness, of six months' duration, caused me
to resign my army chaplaincy, and henceforth " Miss
Kate" was finally severed from the soldiers and their
wives, for whose welfare she had given her labour
and thought, and for whom she had once so resolutely faced Death. Her sphere was now on a
smaller area—some almshouses for decayed trades-
men—where with a quiet, firm hand she soon supplied *wants* which many of the inmates were sorely
tried by. One case may suggest a variety of other
wants : a poor widow maintaining her widowed
sister with a home and food, by starving both
upon some 5*s.* a week, to keep her from the Union,
which would have barred her from an election to
the almshouse ! Another was a mother, very aged

and quite deaf, supporting, on the same pittance, a diseased and suffering daughter, whose husband had cruelly deserted her. The chapel offertories were our fund; a weekly gathering at every service being begun, and a systematic "distribution" made of the alms, and generally in some excess, leaving the chapel account in debt to the chaplain or to " Miss Kate." Her care for the poor alms-people was illustrated by many a service : the sick and suffering found a new order at work. Her relief was, as ever, not by the customary shilling, but was *proportioned* to the special need : *one* might have little; where greater need was, there was greater help; and thus her small funds reached to a considerable sum yearly, in " charity" only—£19—and "nothing was lost," or any overlooked. Whoever was sick, that quiet, gentle footstep soon followed, with the clear, pitying eye and the ever-helpful hand. One poor old alms-woman fell ill, who had been proverbial for her unclean person and rooms; "Miss Kate" got her opportunity; but the first request from the now bed-prisoner was, " O ! mem, don't let her "—a woman-helper sent by us—"' put me to rights,' and don't let her clean me up or wash me !" yet this seemingly sordid soul, *whose neck she thought it scorn to wash for numberless years*, in her illness, remembered, and murmured to me continually, hymns learned and treasured from her far-off youth! At last, by gentle attraction, " Miss Kate " had her way, and the poor aged woman resigned herself and submitted like a child to the younger, loving heart, as if to a mother's breast.

That word " Mother " is not an impossible imagination as used of an elder to a younger. One aged couple—both over 90—joined together for seventy years—were noteworthy. The man an old coast *captain* of a smack, and dredger; the wife a gardener and florist's daughter; always looking like a flower, with her sweet, simple face and snow-white cap. The man was a *character;* blunt, pointed, fearless, with a devotion to his aged wife most touching ; whom to help with an arm no one might presume in his presence—a very knight of chivalrous service, and a man of superior intelligence and strong will. His talk was racy, of the salt of the sea, yet toned by the truest knowledge of Holy Scripture of any man I have met in his social sphere. Of " such a man " I have this memory : " Well, Sir," said he one day, in his strong, emphatic way, " Mrs. Hobson has been a real *mother* to my wife!" The same stern soul on another occasion brought down the silk umbrella of his wedding treasure and lent it to " Miss Kate," with the words, "Seventy years old, mem, but nobody should have it but you." Two *wax* candles, also the wedding furnishing, were the joint gift of man and wife! who could refuse such a present?

She had very many costly gifts from "rich neighbours" and friends, but her numerous offerings from the poor, of no value in themselves, were the most touching—from the "honest and good heart" of the givers. Of these were some things preserved for long years, and here and there some work of hand of man or woman; one was a treasured heir-loom presented with the assurance that "it was my grandmother's, ma'm;" and all such were the poor offerers' return for some help or service to them—men and women—and so was the habitual forwardness of "hands" to aid in her work in any way possible; kindness always seemed to bring kindness. Often and often these relics were the subject of reminiscences, in after days, and of stories of unforgotten troubles—"poor soul, she gave me that the night before leaving for India, begging me to keep it." And here it is! still kept. "Those were some of her pickings at St. Helena, 'Curios,' she called them;" "That was sent home for me by Eliza H.'s husband from Lucknow;" "Poor B. (a schoolmaster), always in trouble, *without shirt in order to help his old mother,*

he came down, crying, to ask me to accept this."
One gift, in 1855, not costly but very precious, is
a few olive-leaves and a flower from Mount Olivet by
Lady N——. They have the signature of the donor,
and to me are a sanctity of our Lord's Agony, and
a memento of the suffering at Kululi, *where they were
presented.*

At this period a new service claimed " Miss Kate "
—the Orphanage of the " Sisters of the Church " at
Kilburn; and this work she ceased not, till the
illness which ended in the "new life" of the Paradise
of God. Funds were, as always, wanting, and the
response to appeals for cast-off clothes for the
orphans, and for sale, had been so exuberant that to
dispose of the stock was an unthought of difficulty.
" Miss Kate " saw a way, and had bales of things
sent down to her. At first her sales were private ;
to friends, for charitable disposal in their own
localities ; but soon the matter was reported and
applicants rushed forward, some on the chance of
selling again with profit for themselves. Then,
sales were announced at her own house, and a
large gathering of eager expectants—*all with ready
money*—came once or twice a week. The sales came
off on the lawn, weather permitting. Heaps and

H

heaps of clothing were laid out, and each purchaser came to "Miss Kate" for the price of everything. Rigid order was established without difficulty, and no *time* was wasted. There was no questioning of the price allowed. It was known that every article was a *bargain*, and, the rule being known, there was never, or *very* seldom, the slightest demur or attempt at reducing the price. Some very rare cases of misconduct occurred when, out of the miscellaneous crowd of towns-people, some *one* would forget the private garden, and that she was not dealing with a shopkeeper, or in a common market, but, with the audible approval of the majority, the offender would be firmly dismissed from the premises. In "Miss Kate's" account-book I find these illustrative entries —"Sale on lawn, two hours, £16;" "Sale on lawn, one hour, £21 15*s*. 3*d*." It was a lively time at those sales! Eager, poor mothers with practical eyes, knowing "what was what," and "good for the use" of family needs; careful wives, with keen glances at a gentleman's coat or other garment for a working-man's Sunday robe, and many other purchasers. There was quickness and keenness so intense that the huge piles of garments, of all kinds, for man, woman, child, disappeared like a beggars' feast, and all were satisfied, knowing that price and real worth were out of all proportion, and profit on the contrary side from common barter and sale.

Besides this provision for the poor, at home, " Miss Kate" had *correspondent* purchasers far and near; many of them friends, who for many a poor and remote parish or locality were glad to make good bargains : even lady friends were also sharers of the benefit. Valuable jewels and trinkets of all kinds; whatever, in short, might make money, had been brought into the net; costly rings, old watches, brooches, seals, bracelets, relics of the past or self-denying offerings of the present. One entry is " Sister V.'s earrings, £2 2*s.* ;" and not a few *presents*, to some friend or kindred passed away, came from the varied store ; and to obtain gifts as choice as cheap being an irresistible chance, some, whose limited means would else have failed to measure their generous thought, were enabled to *give* within their means to some dear one.

Then, after the whole town and vicinity had become familiar with the facts, a public sale was held periodically—in a large hired room—where helpers, young and old, assisted as sellers. All prices were marked, or, where not marked, they were referred to " Miss Kate," and she, standing by the door (to prevent the taking off of things not paid for), examined each bundle, and, with marvellous ease and rapidity, would tell up big and little purchases; the number of articles, not seldom ranging from a few to forty or fifty, at all prices—a few pence, to larger sums in silver or gold.

Simultaneously with this country work " Miss Kate " got up sales in London at public rooms; when supporters of the Orphanage, fair girls and matron-ladies, aided, as at bazaars (without their objectionable features and excitement), and large sums were thus obtained more than once, though sometimes, it was found, at an expense too heavy in proportion to the extra sales. The remains of the London material, specially the clothing, were brought down for disposal publicly to the country folk.

Of course all this involved enormous labour; not only on sale-days but in preparation for such : for there was the assorting of goods; tacking prices to each article; packing and unpacking the bales; valuing; choosing for special orders and wants; the despatch of endless parcels to the surrounding country, and to distant places by rail, and the *keeping of accurate accounts.*

This is all very simple drudgery to read about, and so is the " Garden-party " device. There was nothing brilliant or smart in the idea; but, like Columbus' legendary egg, nobody else had thought of it ; and so, "Miss Kate's" advice to the Sisters, to open a depôt for sale by retail daily—as in an ordinary shop —was alike an obvious track to strike out ; and the marvellous development of this branch of the good Sisters' work, in many places in town, is beyond all previous hope, and the poor men and wives appreciate the benefit abundantly, from East London and the Docks to Kilburn northward.

CHAPTER XIV.

—✠—

"Without haste, without rest."—*Göethe.*

HO is sufficient for these things? might be asked; and the reply is that there required a heart engaged for the orphanage and the poor; method; cool intensity; a talent of prevision and provision, with a real gift of order, and a power of *incessant working;* and these were all as natural qualities in this servant of the poor and of her Lord. Moreover, with wondrous self-control, there was the singular—almost mysterious—*calm* that ever shone in her spiritual eyes, and spake of divine depths of inspiring grace making her labours to be "without haste, without rest." The deepest and sweetest tranquillity of look, manner, and conviction were apparent to all, and irresistible. No amount of work appalled; no demand of continued exertion moved her. *Ever,* as far and as truly as I may judge, she was *occupied;* in thought or act, and in her most silent moods she was brooding over some soul's need, or some desirable end; which a sudden word or question would reveal to me, in a soft, firm voice, with that settled look of loving light and

thought, and the simple response, " O I was thinking
of that poor Mrs. ——;" or, " What is to become of
that girl E——;" or, " I wonder if one might get
so and so to do such and such a thing;" or, perhaps
with no word from me, she would break the silence
by the frequent form, " Dear, I wish you would just
make out a little note of ——;" or, " I wish you
would write to ——;" that is, to promote some work,
or get some help.   In all which silent movement
there was the proof of life's paramount occupation,
the service of " the divine Master."   It was ever

" Condo et compono quæ mox depromere possim[a] ; "

and, hence, her action—well thought out—bare the
strain of practical working; with a very infrequent
need of altering the first design.   Whatever she
undertook there seemed to spring up quickly a vital
force, vivifying the necessary routine and throwing
off waste and impractical elements of action, and
bringing to the front reality and earnestness in others.
Clever people are not seldom impractical, but she was
vitally practical.   She had no room for " pottering "
people [b], or those " whose fingers were all thumbs."

[a] " I lay up and construct what I may soon set forth."—*Horace.*
[b] Her practical temper was touched almost to wrath on the
night before leaving for the Crimea.   She had been hard at

She " meant business " in her action, as much as any eager trader. No wonder then that during her charge of the selling "business" she gathered up in eight years, by all means public and private, some £2,300 for the Orphanage.

More private action was never wanting : trouble, like an electric cloud, ever seemed to be attracted to the ready-helper. A poor alms-woman, in great need, had help from " Miss Kate," and soon, in an unmeant confidence, she mentioned her cousin, Mr.——, a man of great wealth, then recently dead. She had for years (living unknown to him not far from his " place ") borne the sharpest poverty, and was now near the wealthy widow's residence, but had *never made herself known or asked for help.* For years she had been at starvation point, keeping off the parish, as so many poor do, even unto starving, till sickness came, and with it God's fit messenger, who felt that help might be had. It was not an easy or desirable mission, but the rich relation was, pro-videntially, " Miss Kate's " friend, and so the poor work all day, and, in the early hours of the morrow—three o'clock—she was sent for by the " Mother Superior," and had to go *through an open space* to her rooms (in November), and there heard that she was sent for to be shown the particular bead which the Mother had reserved in her rosary to remember her by !

one was, with honouring confidence in the former, brought to her knowledge; and the end was that " Miss Kate" was asked to name a proper weekly allowance, and to dole it out to her patient. It is, of course, quite easy to "pooh pooh" action like this; but " go and do likewise," Objector, and then, and not before, come back, *successful*, and say the task was easy. I doubt if the fact of a warm friendship between the agent and the wealthy benefactor of the poorer sister did not make the risk greater, success more doubtful, and the way of proceeding more difficult; for friendship has most delicate obligations and instincts, and to force attention to an unwelcome subject—and with a *money* claim as the issue—is often felt as an unfair advantage, and strains the silken bond to breaking quickly. That *one* soul, here, was nobly generous, and the other lovingly sincere, and "quick to feel and wise to know" may account for the perfect accord and an increased mutual affection. The burthen rolled off one overweighted life was the amplest reward to both, and the solace to " Miss Kate" unspeakable; but she was neither physically nor morally "a coward," and this moral facing of possible pain and estrangement may be another stroke of truth's hammer towards her statue.

Years before the time just referred to a friend, Governor of the Bank of England and of untold wealth, used to ask "Miss Kate" about sundry "cases" for relief (and his gifts, or alms, were large), but he had an aversion to be first moved from without; such intrusion generally drawing his purse-strings tight against a case. On a *poor* officer's daughter being about to be married, whose family was large, the kindly *Dives* came for advice or consultation—"I am a little puzzled what sort of wedding-present to make." There was a little conferring about circumstances and prospects, and the point was gained at last. "*Might* I, then, give a sum of money?" "By all means," was "Miss Kate's" instant reply, "and I am sure it will be the more valued for the practical sense and kindly consideration so shown." The gift followed, on the wedding morning—a cheque for a hundred guineas !

"Who *dares*, wins—or honour or success."

More trying to endure and longer than that of the poor woman in a previous paragraph, was a case of enormous misery which befel a widowed mother of four children. Vice and a weak nature, abused through the pressure of an accidental official power, brought ruin upon two souls. The woman, who for good services of herself and husband to government had received a pension, lost it and her situation; and the man, also in an important office, with certain prospects of improvement, was degraded from his office and suffered pecuniarily to his ruin. Like a thunder-clap the first news came, and I started off to seek out the unhappy woman, whom I found hidden in our modern Babel, *sheltered, with the four children* (despite of disgrace and utter indigence), by a former neighbour, and who knew *all* the infirmity, the accursed wiles, the fascination that paralysed the will, and the hopeless future; and yet took in a sister victim, and shared her house with her! I got her an office, telling her case, but well was it, though of impossible prevision, that a fine, smart and shrewd Scotchman knew of *our* interest in the widow; and also knew all the misery, yet for "auld lang syne," they said, would marry her! Him we helped to a good position, which he kept for many years, even till now; and a year of peace and rest was secured to the sufferer; but, alas! within two years the end came, and *four* orphans were "Miss Kate's" voluntary charge, under a death-bed prayer for *some* care for them, such as might be possible, and, with which, the poor mother died in peace. Quickly, all the four were put into orphanages, and school ; and the way of the future was unrevealed. " Miss Kate," ordered all things that concerned them for years (with some pecuniary help from their good grandmother whilst she lived), till the two elder were, with measurable ability, but unmeasurable and mischievous *pride*, able to provide for themselves, though the hereditary vice and uncontrollable tempers were the cause of shipwreck to more than ordinary opportunities on many occasions, and were a grief to their protector and benefactor. The third child did well, and is still of good report ; but the fourth was of an wholly indescribable character. She could be as good as gold, and as wicked as a possessed one ! strong as an ox, clever, sensitive to beauty, advanced in the use of pencil and brush ; open to warm affection for her " mother " (as she lightly said, *by her real mother's coffin*, " Miss Kate " should be), yet liable to sudden gusts of passion and violence that hindered the most patient and repeated helps provided for her ; whom no tenderness of a " mother's " care restrained, when " the fever was upon her ; " yet penitent, weeping and prostrate after the tempest-fit had passed, and *alway clinging to her one refuge.*

Such a responsibility few would have been equal to, or could have continued to acknowledge ; a

wearying anxiety, with no respite and no sustaining
motive, but the promise to the dying mother, and
the hope of final benefit to the children.   After a
few years there was added the smart pressure of the
pecuniary burthen ; for, through an astounding per-
fidy and broken pledge, on the faith of which I had,
by best advice, resigned my benefice, I was deprived
of *all* my Church income, and " Miss Kate " was in
some strait to provide for the orphans (one at a
training college), and was reduced—in silent resolu-
tion that would not give up her charge—to provide
the expense, in a great measure, by her needlework
in wools, and embroidering, and other handiwork,
whose sale supplied the means of continuing her
help.

A Statue has some advantage over a painting ; but
there are some things of the "inner man" that
neither one nor the other is equal to.   Words have
this advantage over both, that they may sculpture
even the most latent and intangible action and
powers of the soul ; and so the " unconquerable will,"
without external sign or visible suffering, finds its
place in the moral statue : As in the pest at Kululi,
so now, " Miss Kate," like Charles Gordon, might be
overcome and die, but *she could not throw aside her
trust.*

CHAPTER XV.

——✠——

"The day was now far spent."... "This is a desert place."
—*S. Mark* vi. 35.
"And he went ... into the wilderness ... and sat down
under a juniper tree: and he requested ... that he might
die."—1 *Kings* xix. 4.

UPON a Hampshire heath, with wide flats of
sponge-like bog amid higher ground of sandy
hills of pine, "Miss Kate" was now thrown perforce.
Poor little C——! with waters, above and below,
stopping exit in winter's floods, and isolated from any
town population; it seemed now that the *sales* of
past years must fall through, and the organizer, like
the prophet, might despair. Nor was there wanting
temptation to go away from the locality where a foul
evil and ruinous injury had been wrought, and we
sufferers were "strangers in the land." Silent and
tranquil was the way of one soul, but *curæ leves
loquuntur graviores silent*[a], and, with no outward show,
such an opprobrium sank deeply into the thought, and
burned inwardly with a sure force, weakening and
wearing down, albeit unconsciously, the whole system

[a] "Small troubles cry out; great ones are still."—*Seneca.*

of mind and body, telling gradually (and the more as the day was "now far spent," and the hidden end near) upon the always fragile health, and accelerating disease in her who was ever moved to intensity by any iniquity, oppression, or false action. It is only higher souls that suffer beyond what "our coarser natures know;" and the higher the grace the more vital the suffering, even as no man, or even angel, can fully realize what the presence of sin was to our Lord!

Still the end was not yet; even in a wilderness of spiritual and physical want and barrenness God can stay the soul and feed with His own hand and providence both soul and body, and say to His servant, "go forth on the way." Even out-of-the-way C—— had a brief visitation of goodness, and an out-shining of light and life to the poor and needy, beyond their ordinary lot. We had a sort of Swiss châlet, withdrawn amid the heath of glorious furze and gorse— and such flowery exuberance of these as elsewhere I never saw; enough to make Linnæus shout with rapture! Here, in a little while, the unused pony-stable was filled with bales of sacking, stuffed to the point of bursting, and, the way from the railway to the house being through the village, great was the wonder there at such an unwonted sight, and as to what the new

clergyman was going to do with such big boxes,
portmanteaus, packing-cases, and such heaps of some
soft things rolled together, and sown up against
inspection, yet looking like the "flitting" of a poor
man's bed and bedding. At last the secret was out,
through the bursting of one of the sacking bales.
"Why it's clothes!" said one porter; "Yah," said
another, "and them are *old ones;*" and the news was
soon heard in every house; and then the new parson's
man, at the chapel he had come to take up on H——
Hill, told all about the work, and the sales to follow.

"Miss Kate's" usual lot was her portion here.
Help to unstitch, uncord, and empty the contents
of boxes, sacking, and other holders of goods, was
necessary, beyond what the house could supply, but
there was no cottage or other house near save a hut
and its one-storied neighbour; yet it so befel that an
old couple, hale and knowing, occupied the former,
and a room off this was let to us, where also stores
of material were stowed. Here was found what was
wanted; the man and the fine and good old wife
were just at hand, able and honest as the day—
barring the report of some youthful poaching, the
ineradicable sign of manhood, from Nimrod downward—and were as willing as able, of free choice
and without pay, to help in every way. Then, for

a day or two it was incessant labour, disgorging huge piles of clothes, the careful sorting of which was " Miss Kate's " work solely. When the things were ready there was no need of bellman or " posters ; " the fact spread like the heath fires from the lonely house over the whole country side for miles. One great purchaser, who came to every sale to the last, was found to be a dealer from Aldershot —four miles away—driving her own donkey-cart, and supplying things, at a profit, to soldiers and their wives. Others came, some in carts and some walking, from many a solitary heath and far-away place. One woman trudged nine miles for the chance of good purchases for her "long" family ; so quick were the poor souls to see the profit and seize upon the opportunity of the sales.

It was a sight when the day of sale came, and a hundred and more women, with now and then a man, gathered in the midst of abundance of goods spread out in great mounds, or selected in smaller portions, on the grassy garden-plat. The eager interest, the quick perception of what each wanted, the glad payment (and *thanks* generally added) were a study. Very knowing were most women as to the particular article sought and its shop value ; but they were *not* skilled in measurements, and

again and again one and another would bring up
shyly to "Miss Kate" a coveted lady's dress, or
outer jacket, mantle, or other robe, and ask if she
thought it would *fit;* when, in a minute, with a quick
glance, the figure would be caught, and "yes" or
"no" infallibly pronounced, with ready help if
needed to some other *real fit* when possible. "Infallible" is a potent word, but it is certain that an
eye for proportion, and a vast experience, had done
for "Miss Kate" what long training enables a clever
shopman to do for a customer at a glance ; and her
measure scarcely ever—if ever—failed. Many would
watch and wonder at the rapidity of the choice and
the unerring decision as to the *fit;* it was truly a
gift—what God gives to humble and believing builders
for Him, as to Bezaleel and Aholiab in the building
and ornamentation of the Tabernacle in the wilderness [a].

During this time of making the Hampshire heaths
smile with joy at the good things brought within reach
of the poorest, "Miss Kate" also continued the

[a] Very real was the gratitude of the poor people of C——, for
on hearing of a "Friends' Memorial Window" being proposed
to their helper, they (after four years' lapse) asked the lady
who kept on the Mothers' Meeting if, "without offending," they
might send their coppers to me, which of course were thankfully received and valued, as the widow's mite.

sales in London, and, being nearer, was able to flit
up and down more frequently to the Orphanage,
where all the stores were, jammed in rooms *hardly*
got at by her weakening steps. In hopeless confusion the good Sisters were perforce content to
leave the unknown treasures till the deliverer came.
Looking at the mass of things before her, heaped
up to the very roof, she, never daunted, never doubting, would smile thankfully ; and at once, in a method
known to herself only, she would steadily attack
and take away from the chaotic pile such things
as her country poor most wanted ; and busily were
the orphan girl-workers kept at the task of stitching
up the packages, cording the boxes, and hammering
the nails roughly into packing-cases, till, in a wondrously short time, the mighty accumulations showed
huge gaps, and the room would sensibly grow lighter,
and more airy, by their removal outside the house,
where awaited the van to cart them away to the
station, or, after a more careful provision for a town
sale, including the usual supplies of a bazaar, to
the public room hired for the sales.

CHAPTER XVI.

"but 'tween
Our shadowings and their end doth intervene
One that doth love us, shaping all for good."—*I. Williams.*

"Homo proponit sed Deus disponit."—*Thomas à Kempis.*

SOONER than expected the place of our rest was to be changed : the châlet was put up for sale, and I at once took time by the forelock, and sought another home for the now more than ever suffering worker. Her strength was reduced by much pain; her cough would go on through the night without respite; continual sickness following and blood-spitting, by some lesion of the smaller vessels, through the harrowing strain on the chest; and there were other complications; yet, after such a night, without rest, without sleep, ever seeking relief from the sickness, weary and worn, she would yet rise calmly and patiently [a], and, though rain might

[a] It is proverbial that men are sooner depressed by sickness than women, and it is marvellous how those who are habituated to suffering learn patience. or, at least, are less moved to depression than those who are habitually in good health. The

pour, drive to the station, two miles, and go off by
train to some sale in town already prepared ; and
there, standing about, ordering, and having the
general charge, she would be at work till night ; and
then, with the remains of unsold goods to pack, she
and her helpers would finish the day's work with
the *"reckoning"* of what had been taken, and, well
nigh broken down, she would seek for necessary
repose at the Orphanage, to awake next morning
and carry off to the country the unsold things. Often
have I been astonished at the indomitable will and
resolute perseverance that carried her through any
undertaking once begun, always assured, through
humble trust and self-forgetfulness, that " as thy day
so shall thy strength be."

A singular instance of the characteristic here named
occurred some fourteen years ago. A dear friend,
at thirty-two, had nine children, and the doctors
forbad her any more nursing. There was a con-
sulting of ways and means and persons, when " Miss
Kate " settled the perplexity by undertaking for the
coming baby herself, and this was how it was done.

reason is the same : women suffer more frequently than men,
and so are not moved as by something *strange;* and it is the
unaccustomed that makes the hale folks too soon cast down.
Men and healthy people realize a *loss* which the others do not.

She provided a nurse, known to her and near to us, and when the "hour was come" she was present and ready, and took the little freshlet from the mother's first embrace, and ran off with her, like the fairies of olden story, to the train and home—some seventy miles—where the nurse was waiting to carry her into the foster-mother's family, a couple of miles more. The daring and "strange device" succeeded perfectly. The child grew and waxed strong, and "was in the desert," nourished with an alien's strength, till she grew to be indeed " a proper child" and " fair," with rustic ways and skin darkened by sun and wind, and "roughing it" as one of the labourer's own family. Her first visit to us, ere taken home, when able to sit at table, was distinguished by an act that opened widely several pairs of eyes. She suddenly took up her plate and *licked* it openly, till exclamations and laughter surprised her in the very act, when, with unconscious innocence, holding still the plate in her hand, she simply *stared* with mute inquiry ! The dear child had been baptized, and like all her sisters had a flower name, " Mign-onette " (shortened into " Mignon "), and " Miss Kate," of course, was one of her godmothers ; who ever kept up the spiritual relationship, and sent her frequent gifts of childish interest. She has now grown into girlhood, and her large, shy, wondering eyes and healthy looks are no longer unrefined from rusticity.

Thus another of " Miss Kate's " adventures of love prospered, but it was a common remark with her most intimate friends, " whatever she does it prospers." In our frequent removes she had her store of bulbs carefully sorted and kept, as some one's gift, or other memento — Russian violets brought home by herself—and in her still way she would, at odd moments, put them into the ground, and, despite of all adverse influences, they were always sure to grow; and yet she never seemed to take any special pains or concern about them. Like S. Francis, who could talk with birds and flowers, she seemed to have a secret understanding with nature, and nothing of hers " fell to the ground " to die away. She was the very opposite of *Lalla Rookh*, who " never loved a tree or flower but 'twas sure to die."

But the secret process of life may not pause, and He, who orders all in His good providence, saw that her time of departure was drawing near, albeit hidden to mortal eyes; and knowing that " the journey was too great " for her, overruled our removal that she might have a tranquil home at eventide; and so,

after my many journeyings here and there, such a
home was found, in a most unlooked for way. Many
a time in other days, passing from Dover by the London and Chatham line, I had noted, just out of the
suburbs, a locality that few can see without admiring.
In a deep valley, where the *Dour* rises, the line
passes a mansion, of *modern* building, now called
Kearsney *Abbey*, lying very low upon a still piece
of water, and half-buried among stately trees. All
around are hills some 600 feet high, wooded, or
where old common lands remain, covered with furze.
Years before I had walked hence to *Deal*, and found,
on rising out of the valley, a table-land of wide cir-
cumference, through whose once level area the Dour
and numerous other valleys are cut, as the spaces
between the fingers of a hand, all trending to ancient
Dover; a most singular and picturesque conforma-
tion of country, offering walks in every direction, and
always beautiful; with glintings, down the valleys, of
the blue sea and the French coast by Cape Gris-nez.
The village of *Temple Ewell* is here, at the head of
the springs of the Dour; and here was our home
to be! One day I had gone to Ramsgate and elsewhere searching for a house, and meaning to take
Temple Ewell on my way back, but, being detained
too long, I had to miss my visit, but, not being will-

The Old Parsonage.

" Lovely nest, in which your ' bonniest Bird of God ' folded her wings at last."

ing to omit the chance of such a situation, I wrote
from Davington Priory, Faversham, where I was staying, to the Vicar—as an entire stranger—telling my
want, and received a reply that took me down to see
a *villa*, which "is not a villa," but, as he said, has
"a character of its own;" and I at once hired it on
lease ; and certainly not even a poet's home need be
more quaintly poetical. At an angle made by an
ancient bridle-road to Sandwich and Deal with the
old pilgrim-road to Canterbury ; with 305 feet front-
ing the latter, covered with a flowering creeper—
the "travellers' joy," or wild clematis—on an ele-
vation of some 20 feet above the carriage-way, the
"old parsonage" and its garden are notably distinguished from "villa" architecture. Built some hundred and fifty years ago, its walls are a foot and a half
thick. On the slope of a hill, also, it has to conform
to the angle of the outside road (the rooms being
squared inside by closets at one end), and also to
the rise of the ground—the drawing-room being some
12 feet higher than the lower rooms, dining-room and
study,—and the two former opening alike by French
windows upon a small lawn and garden. Caves in
the solid chalk form the cellars, where a deep unfailing well of coldest and purest water is forced to the
upper rooms. By knocking two sleeping-rooms into

one I made "Miss Kate" an airy night abode—
23 feet by 12½—and the dining and drawing-rooms
are of similar dimensions. Surrounded by hills, with
a south-western aspect, every cold wind is avoided,
and our shelter is perfect. A row of shining beech
run their lateral arms over the road past the house,
at the distance of the width of the highway. The
"village and the village church," and all the hills,
appear from the windows, and below, in the valley,
sparkles and hurries on the infant Dour, and many
a "cottage by the brook" is literally the fact.

Here then was, providentially, her last remove.
Here she was to "rest from her labours!" The two
years at C—— had been a time of increasing weakness, albeit with little outward sign, and concealed
from many eyes by unflagging activity in the cause
of the Orphanage; about which the good and gentle
Mother Superior wrote, "Your dear wife was one of
our oldest and most valued friends. She did most
lasting work for us, and she gave us both her time
and her thought;" but, alas! that which mere physical disease and suffering alone might not so soon
have wrought, it is probable that her great *moral*
sensitiveness brought about. She with myself had
had her work stopped at our H—— charge, after
our many months of action in arrangements and

provisions of various kinds : she, to whom anything
pertaining to sickness and nursing was a life experience; and an impracticable woman, with no one
reason but a crazed wilfulness, without a word of
difference or explanation—to such an one—set aside
every engagement wildly; and even showed despite
unto one to whom Joshua Hopper, a rich city man's
daughter, should have done genuine homage. To
my sufferer this was a matter of calm contempt, but
I felt it even more than my own treatment—she,
valued, revered, beloved, beyond ordinary experience, to be set at nought by the annoyance of an
evil wilfulness. It would have been more than
human that the shock of disappointment should
have had no effect upon her thought; even whilst
silent and seemingly unmoved. But the force of
the *moral* suffering to her was not in its direct personal effects upon her or myself: it was beyond all
mere personal element, and awoke in her a *horror*
not to be described. As before mentioned, she was
ever deeply moved by any paltering with truth;
unfaithfulness to a trust; pandering to wrong doing;
or shirking of duty; and specially when another
suffered injury or loss from the offence; and, alas !
all these were in the web of cunning and treachery
woven by a woman and a lawyer, and justified by

a priest; the latter the most fearfully responsible, as being her spiritual *director*, whom she desired to place in virtual control of her new chapel and "Home," rather than him who was her husband's choice. The lawyer, after my first and only interview, I privately denounced in her sister-in-law's house, where she was staying, as an unmistakeable rogue, in my conviction; which, by an unequalled failure and flight from the country, he soon appeared to be; at a loss to the woman and her connections of sums of money ruinously large; but the swift nemesis was not undeserved, and it was so direct and conspicuous that it struck many; the injurious were injured; the covenant breakers were betrayed; the abusers of power were abused, and the wilfully arrogant were overridden and set at nought. "I will repay, saith the Lord," and it was so.

It was a stupendous break-up of, it was said, a million or more, and yet one dared not rejoice at the punishment of any thereby; but rather grieved over the *moral* infatuation that had invited the retribution; yet such an evil experience was not easily shaken out of the thoughts: it haunted the memory, after all connections had ceased; and "Miss Kate" would sometimes say, "What a mystery that such evil is permitted." So it was with other wickedness.

At the story of Jael she never failed to shudder : all the tenderness of her womanly nature, and her divine pity, were shocked at the action, and she would say, " I cannot bear it ; I cannot understand it." Once, only a little while before her departure, she thus spake of Jael, when it occurred in the Bible-reading, and I then quickly—in our life's repose—led her to see the story in the lights of Eastern thought and manners, and as an unpremeditated act of sudden unaccountable impulse, and perhaps fear of her woman's responsibility for harbouring a man, and she was soothed, if not perfectly understanding. There were in fact two currents within her soul, and the sphere of her faith was not vitally touched by such perplexities. She suffered from the contemplation of all evil done, but the two elements of doubting revulsion as to right, and of true *faith*, were separate forces with her, and no amount of the former diminished or dimmed the latter. The one was of the understanding and a pure conscience ; the other was a concrete life of dependence on a person ; a relationship, communion, and vital consciousness, beyond the reach of any earthly perplexities to disturb or distract. It was an analogue of the physiological fact of nerves of sight and feeling, and of the brain's functions, that trench not upon their

opposites, though in one organ and matter.   Blessed
is the gift of such *faith*, and happy are they who
by it begin even on earth to live the very eternal
life of God.

CHAPTER XVII.

—✠—

"Or ever the silver cord be loosed, or the golden bowl be broken."—*Eccles.*

"Here in this quiet nook."

UR first year at Temple Ewell was one of extraordinary heat, in the summer when we arrived; and she suffered greatly—more than ever she had before at home or in the East—the *exhaustion* being felt day and night; and an unwonted perspiration with oppression at the chest were altogether most painful to witness. In the later autumn she had grievous anxiety with the youngest of the orphans before mentioned. She was, and would, if possible, be with her "mother," yet could not restrain herself from occasional savage outbreaks. Her sister's presence with us, on a visit to see her, caused one of these gusts, through an evil jealousy; and this trial became so intense, and the fits so frequent, that it might not continue, for the effects were now more visible and wearing to the "mother" than of old; and as the mad young thing was suddenly drawn to the UNION, to that we took her (all other homes having been in turn forfeited), yet, though going *there of choice* to be with paupers, at the last moment, on being told to get up on the box-seat with the village driver of the carriage, she whirled round on her heel and declared *she* " was not going to ride in front !" Only my interference, and a threat which she feared as worse than the box-seat, induced her to yield. Alas ! in a couple of months, after several præmonitions, the "mother" was required to remove her (for whom she had duly paid) for wild and insubordinate conduct, being guilty of mounting on the roof of the " house," and of other high freaks.

Another year of cessation from all laborious work, with power only to help in near and indoor matters, passed, and the sufferer could take occasional walks, and sometimes she would drive for a "rapture" of contemplation to the sea—" a joy for ever" to her— where, at Dover, old military friends were once or twice successful in getting her to some garden party ; but her debility grew more and more, and her fingers more feeble, yet still she kept on, helping with her vast store of ancient texts, wrought of old with such marvellous ease and rapidity for Church feasts, too soon, alas ! to be given up. Yet twice she got up to town on some service of ministry, and she was able to go to a nine o'clock Holy Communion occasionally and with suffering ; yea, once I note a journey to Wantage (in September, 1855) at which I almost rebelled ; only that I knew her safe-keeping was so habitual, and her own instinct of trust was so divine a gift, that I ever *feared* to oppose, and so let her go, with prayer and blessing. One of her orphans was at the training-school there, towards whom the good Sister in charge had shown much tact and feeling [a]. To help, therefore, on a special occasion was a delight and no small encouragement to the Sister and the orphan.

The next year was one of gradual failure. A rare drive, up to July 1886, but "suffering excessively" was my record in August ; and only few receptions of the blessed Sacrament, though *always* hoping and preparing, and only yielding to remain away at the very last moment. In September she has " fallen

[a] " It was in the autumn of 1885 (writes the Sister in charge) that she was last with us, taking part in and contributing largely to a sale of work that we had for raising funds to enlarge our house. . . . She was quite a marvel to me in her generous self-sacrifice for us who were comparative strangers, and her loving zeal for others' good. There will be many, I doubt not, to rise up and call her blessed ; what she did for the G——'s alone (the orphans) is *a history in itself.* I was struck with her wonderful energy and power of work when she was looking terribly ill, and torn to pieces by a most distressing cough."

K

from the sofa stupified with pain, sickness, &c. ;" and
very soon after this, on trying to work some festal
text, I have the touching gentle cry, " I *cannot.*
I suppose I shall never be able to do another;" and
my secret record of anguish was, " Oh ! oh ! " Was it
wrong to weep secretly ?

The poor hand, once so wondrous in its " cunning,"
by this time is helpless for writing or working, and
the last attempt and resource was the device of
a piece of mere knitting with large wooden needles,
which remains as she left it—a sad memento of my
watching over her feeble action.

During the following year the feebleness was such
that she was not able to get out for Communion save
once, when a Bath-chair was used, and only twice was
she able to go, with assistance, a few yards upon the
upper lawn. Before the end of the year *I* began to
have much suffering and symptoms not understood,
and against all my life's experience, whilst she still
got downstairs; but sad and sore were the scenes of
nightly difficulty in getting the sufferer back to her
bed, out of which she would often fall unconscious.
Yet, agonizing as it was to me, I felt that that *will*,
so nobly strung of old, must be respected ; and that
there was even benefit to her to feel that *all* her
action and habits were not stricken unto death, so

long as she had even so much power. One fall out
of her chair prone upon the floor, cutting her dear
face, was a further sign of the coming end; and yet
there was a respite : after living for some time almost
without food, till nature could bear no more, she
strangely rallied, as the Indian summer, and was able
to be drawn in her chair, and to enjoy the blessed
fresh air, but, most of all, with rejoicing, I saw her
eating again, and she, whose life of watching the sick
had made her always have only cat's sleep, began to
sleep like a child; nothing disturbed her : I might
move her, adjust her sleeping dress about her chest,
or her pillow, or put my hand upon her without
a sign of disturbance; even a moderate shake did
not wake her. Then I began to build a place for
an ass or pony to take her farther away than a man
might, on our hill and vale locality, habitually ac-
complish, however willing the most devoted of servants was. Alas! the change was fallacious. The
Master was secretly, above human ken, calling His
servant to "go up higher."

But we knew it not; His will inscrutable! We
had hoped that she again would go to the Father's
house for Holy Communion at early morning. Failing this, after often hindrances from violent cough or
other suffering, I said the work must be mine, at

home; but, again, it might not be, till the half-cher-
ished hope of Christmas Communion in church was
obliged to be laid aside, and then, on Christmas
Day, I gave her, with another "faithful" soul, her last
Communion privately, at which I first felt my own
disease coming on more sharply, with shortness of
breath and weakened voice; and thenceforward *I
could (save by unceasing prayer) no longer do anything
for the sufferer.* Then the offices of an aged friend
were grateful, in reading to her and saying a prayer;
albeit, sometimes, with her imperfect consciousness
of the action, as it appeared. The Vicar also so
ministered to her, in my hopeless helplessness.

The end was nearer than we thought. I had
rejoiced unspeakably on her summer revival, and the
star of my life's eventide was hope. We had not
realized, weighed, and measured the signs of our
sundering lives: deeper than all exterior things was
our oneness; and assent was as if it were to "continue for ever." So, alas! we all err; deferring that
which is unwelcome; letting slip the unbearable;
shirking the inevitable, till a loving Father wakes
us to reality with an irresistible voice, and we feel
as " in a dream when one awaketh!"

What proved to be the final relapse, the irrecover-
able departure of my earthly blessing, had appeared

in the autumnal change, when a mysterious sympathy with the fading world without so often shows its subtle power. The appetite was again lost, and the sleep, so strange and sweet for a little while, was no more a sensible blessing. Pain and unrest; whole nights of coughing, sickness and prostration, even unto utter helplessness; and, at last, the sufferer would sit for the most part, in chair or bed, without speaking, for hours; but with a fixed gaze, a pale expectant aspect, as if she heard or saw what was beyond those who were watching her so lovingly: resting on her elbow, her left hand raised—in an old habitual posture—towards the cheek, and the fingers feebly moving; when a sudden question would make her start, as if the mind had been in a far-off land; but the relapse was instantaneous; the failing body was evidently overweighing the mind, and sometimes, for a moment, "those that look out of the windows were darkened." What passed around her, all unremarked, had ceased to move her, and she who long—

> " . . . with eye illumined, soft, serene,
> Had caught each tone in earth, and sea, and sky,
> And made fair memories of Life's fleeting scene "—

grew gradually apathetic to outward influences; and upon the void silence came only an infrequent " voice

of words," that sadly told of a cloud stealing over
even the mind's action, through the mere pressure of
bodily derangement and physical decay.   There was
no anxiety apparent at last, save for the faithful servant's presence, whose help was so grateful, and
whose gentleness was touching.   *He* only could
move her as she wished, and give her passing relief.

Neither were there any *painful* wanderings of
disordered thought; no mental visionings " babbling
of green fields," or inward conflict such as saintliest
souls have often felt[b]; it was sheer breaking down

[b] The sweet and pure soul of George Herbert had this
conflict at the hour of death, and so had the good and holy
Bishop of Lincoln, recently departed.   Nor should we be
surprized at this.   In the very hour when the Christian Victor
is near to receive his crown, it is not strange that the evil one
should exert his fiercest efforts to arrest his own final defeat.
So it was with "the King of Saints;"   it was upon the Cross
that He suffered what the Greek Church calls His "unknown
agonies," that drew forth His one mystical cry of seeming
despair, " My God, My God, why hast Thou forsaken Me?" It
suits the Church of Rome to descant upon the infallible and unfailing *peace* that she alone can give, as is notably the boasting
assumption of J. H. Coleridge the Jesuit, in the Life of Lady
Georgiana Fullerton, but the truth is otherwise far.   Many
a death-bed of good men and women, and even "religious,"
has attested the power of the evil one even unto the last.   Had
her boast been true, had she really possessed the powers which
she claims over the heart, intellect, and conscience, she had never

of the "wall of the flesh;" and the inner light was overpowered by the inrush of irresistible outward currents; but though her failing sight was steadfastly fixed upon the great Cross of our old Church banner, which I had caused to be hung in the direction of her habitual posture; and its presence doubtless soothed the wearied brain and heart somewhile; and though all pleasant things were around her, as of old, with an aged "sister" also near her, whose singular snow-white shock of hair, as a very aureole, fair to see, was grateful whilst reading or saying some prayer, yet the disturbing forces were not subdued; the discord of consciousness, through the "house of flesh" failing, was now apparent: enough to rend me through and through when it became assured: a mind so bright, so clear, so pure, so toned toward heaven, now to fail and relapse! but oh! how sweet, unspeakably, was the soft, strange look, reliant though enfeebled, that still would fall upon the helping watchers, the faithful soldier, and the dearer heart at times!

Until some few weeks before the end the strong, calm will sustained her in moving downstairs; partly borne by the arm of the tender female attendant

lost in the most part of Europe the *manhood* of Christianity. The fact is that Rome may give peace to some, to many; but she cannot give it with *certainty* to even *one.*

wound around her; partly carried; with many a fall and frequent fear.   Then, with placid resignation—in utter helplessness—she stayed in her chamber and came down no more ! Yet, though powerless as a babe, *in every way*, her sufferings diminished, and the last hour was without "pains of death," and in motionless silence.

So came the end ! there was no special, immediate sign. After keeping her bed altogether *I* had not once seen her ; there passed only the nightly and morning "love," by the true woman that brought it tenderly from each to each ; there was no "*last* good night" consciously to either: for just two days there was no hope, and then, suddenly, I *was* bereaved; bereaved even of my promised sight of her, even once; forbidden to leave my separate room ! So, invisibly, God's "great white-winged angel came and kissed her breath" into the paradise of the Saints ; and only once, in her white and violet coffin, I saw her, laid by my peremptory demand upon my bed, on being borne away to the church—"the gate of heaven"—and to her hallowed grave !

And so death comes to all; sometimes suddenly, sometimes insensibly, stealing upon the heart with gentlest stilling of its weariness, and then——

Then ! Is matter indestructible, without increase,

without diminution? Do millions of years make no change of its essential properties; and is life—by the lowest account the flower and fruit of ordered matter—destroyed? or, say, O atheist, scientist, agnostic, what *is* the secret of life, and its issue? Is a life such as I have touched upon weakly; a life of life-long pains—for hers were "many"—to find no solving from any "wise" men of this world? Is it flicked out without hope, annihilated against nature's *order*? Is it not *worth* puzzling over to give a *rationale* of its being? If not, then, what worth is the splendid array of physical wonders which sustain it? If there be no hope of *reparation*, no *recompense* of noble purpose, self-devotion, suffering inexplicable; no *knowledge* of a hereafter any way; then the world, and all that is therein of sentient rational life, would seem a sport or mockery, or inexpiable *wrong* and madness. Yea, more than this, the infinite *rationality* of creation (God's or Nature's) in "magnifical" provisionings and fashionings, in innumerable contrivances—say the fertilization of orchids, the work of earth-worms—is contradicted by the being of the only *reason* known—whether a creation, or the only result of material forces—for, that that which is the very essence and spirit of creation is *produced only to perish* is unspeakably

irrational and against nature.   No ! we shall not die,
all; for

"...... believe thou oh my soul,
Life is a vision, shadowy of truth ;
And vice and anguish and the wormy grave
The shapings of a dream ...... "—*Coleridge.*

And therefore there is no blackness of darkness about
the death of an Immortal in the flesh.   Though to
the world " their end seemeth to be destruction, yet
they are in peace." They go hence with " a hope full
of immortality," and our Eucharist follows them, for
that God hath " delivered them from the miseries of
this sinful world," and changed their " houses of flesh "
for " a building of God eternal in the Heavens."   The
gloom of our English Christian burials ; the morbid
display of hired trappings, and the expense, even
with the poor, is alike against faith and the words
and spirit of the Prayer-Book, " We give Thee hearty
thanks, Almighty God, for that it hath pleased Thee
to deliver the soul of this our sister out of the miseries
of this sinful world."

The snow of an exceptionally bitter and protracted
winter lay on all the surrounding hills, and on valley
and village church, when village men carried the
creamy-white coffin, with its large violet cross affixed
between violet bands, and her Sister's large iron cross

loose—as soldiers' arms—to remain and mingle with her dust. Some loving choir-boys, remembering graciousness long ago, brought from our old Kentish home their floral cross; and with them the organist of other years (all in cassocks and surplices), went from the house, where my rending heart had, momentarily, uttered its broken farewell words and prayer, and pressed the lips and brow and eyes, no more to meet my own in the flesh. A verse was sung, " Brief life is here our portion," and then a pause, and so alternately along the village way till the church was reached, and, I am told that *there*, with a full church, all was simple, touching, and solemn, but *I* saw nothing *there!* Only 'neath the wintry sky and over the snow-clad ground it was a soothing sight to see that procession (and from my bed I looked out upon it) singing on the way; and then the priest in the old Norman church, vested in cassock and violet stole, as of old; and the white-robed choir; and to hear over her grave the last hymn—

" Now the labourer's task is o'er, "

with its soft refrain,

" Father, in Thy gracious keeping
Leave we now Thy servant sleeping."

One of her life-long dislikes was the gravestone or monument over the dead, as if (she said) folly would bar the way of rising again; and so her grave has only a narrow bordering-stone marking its limits, and a small flat head-stone, twelve inches square, containing no more than the words, "Catharine Leslie Hobson," with a small upright iron cross of fifteen inches resting on an iron semi-circle, arching over the name; the support coloured as porphyry, slightly touched with gold, the cross *vermillion*, according with the blazon of the Knights Templars who gave the village its name.

CHAPTER XVIII.

—✠—

" A pilgrim of the faith is limned here
With dinted mail and russet mantle clad.
   *   *   *   *   *   *
Following the footsteps of the Crucified."—*Anon.*

IT may be allowed to complete my statue, or picture of a life, by here catching up stray threads of memory, and drawing together briefly a few traits not before separately noted in the partial narrative. I am not writing the *life* of one that was perfect, or of one who had not a perpetual sense of her own imperfections; I only aim at a figure faithful to the original, and not common—

"A . . . . woman not too good
For human nature's daily food."—*Wordsworth.*

WILL [a].—Eternal fountain of goodness and of evil; mystery of mysteries; fountain, way, end of visible and invisible things; executor of great deeds; imperfect in every human, perfect only in the divine nature;

[a] I feel how thin is the ice upon which I here tread, but I move freely and fearlessly, faithful to my own ideal of what a "life" should be, and dreading no diminution of love to her in loving hearts.

will, that makes and destroys all virtue ; the vital sin
in all—" His *will* was not to do good ! " Her will was
a perplexing study to me for years. What had not
that will done and enabled her to do and sustain ?
For more than thirty years, in unending works, she
suffered from an unknown, inward disease, thought
to be abdominal cancer, besides others outwardly
manifested. With tears the dear old Bishop (A. G.
Spencer, of Jamaica) said, in 1861, "O that dear
soul, she cannot live with that killing cough;" and
when all had gone and she alone was left in the
war hospital, after suffering from fever till life was
given up, it was the unconquerable will, in so frail
a body, that sustained her to " stand fast," and to
die rather than depart ! Wilfulness, in its common
sense, she had none, whose very twin root is *selfishness* and *pride*. Of the former she had none, not
a selfish wish ; and yet she had a form of wilfulness,
and that not easy to measure or control sometimes ;
there seemed even obstinacy and perverseness, trying
and strange to me in our early years of marriage.
I thought of and saw, perhaps, the self-consciousness
of this in the far-off days of our betrothal, when she
remarked on the solemnity of " surrendering her life
unto another !" Who can tell how hard it was for
such a nature, erect, independent, self-guided, always

to yield to another imperfect human will? Yet it was
her peculiarity that she never sought to impose her
will—apart from a question of moral truth—upon
others. Hers was never an intrusive wilfulness, but
a defensive retreat. She would hold her own will
in her own power, as "master of herself," and she
might not be moved to a change until her own
conviction was satisfied; till she saw an *obligation*
to yield. The surrender was all the more difficult,
and sometimes sorrowful to me, in that her con-
clusions—like a true woman's—only partially rested
upon *reasonings* or argument: they came far more
by intuition; and the hard, close, unrelenting logic
of men she could only impatiently endure ; and if
truth wholly depended upon logic, what ought to
have convinced did not. We, in early days, had
estrangements—never of affection—and she would
be as unrelenting as myself. One such is indicated
in the contemporary verses on the fifth page ;
but, singularly, it never was a *great* matter or a vital
question that thus jarred the harmony of loving
lives. I knew her deepest lines of conviction, as
she mine ; and our thoughts were shared without
reserve on all that was of mutual interest in "the
great things of the law;" and if on the surface—the
very surface—there came at times the counterpoise

of equally strong wills, yet against all this there was an un-*willing* wilfulness, all our life long, so that she would not *choose* for herself, or decide when asked, "Will you go here or there?" "Shall I do this or that?" but habitually replied, "Just as you like," or "If you wish it;" and often it was to my grief that she would not *choose* in what way I might gratify her. Oftentimes, abroad, where we spent long periods in my illnesses, my little carefully-prepared surprizes for a climb; a special landscape view; a visit to some rare shrine, were damped by hers and a mutual friend's pleasant decliner, "as who should say," in reply, "You are very kind, and pray *go*, and come and tell us all about it!" The two women often smiled, provokingly, at the man's enthusiasm, and sat still, or, if consenting, would stop half-way to the highest height, or special point of view, and wait my return, smiling still!

PERSEVERANCE.—"Final perseverance" is a far-off battle-field of two opposing schemes of religion, but I speak not now of the "*Grace* to persevere," in the religious sense. There is a high perseverance of nature—

> "So careless of the single life,
> So careful of the type"—

(says Tennyson), and there is an individual perseverance. It is not the same as *will*, though in mutual relation with that. The former is action; the latter power; they are as a *motion* in machinery, and the *power* that moves. They are separable, often even opposed. Life is full of stories of will-failure, whilst others *will*, but lack proper action. " To will is present with me ; but how to perform that which is good I find not " (Rom. vii. 18). There is, moreover, a perseverance of very common obser-vation, and with small minds. A woman, by the "continual dropping" of a contentious or discon-tented mind, will worry a strong man to distraction ; and overcome, in spite of his resistance. There is a perseverance of mere *habit*, also very common. The poor, even where there is little profession of religion, persevere in a strange, unconscious, in-structive way against the many difficulties and chances of their lives, in a kind that is often almost like a divine *faith* in God's providence ; and there are *habits* which are persevered in—by farmers and others, yea by *all*, and often with small reason—when larger knowledge and experience join in con-demning : and there is the perseverance for redress of some wrong, whose emblem is the parable of the widow's importunity, in the Gospel, with its spiritual side, commended unto all as the prayer of *faith*.

L

In all these, save the last, there is no real principle
or praiseworthy action; perseverance that is worthy
and ennobling is wholly in another rank of higher
minds. PALISSY, the potter, in that wondrous wife-
torturing life, showed the perseverance of genius seeking the graces of beauty and perfect art. FAWCETT,
the public man, "with knowledge at one entrance
quite shut out," yet undaunted, and holding on,
under such a calamity, in the noble strife of his
University career, shows the perseverance of deep
principle and high aim. JOHNSON, the scholar,
poverty stricken and "literally out at heels," yet
independent, exhibits the perseverance of self-re-
liance and conscious power, that was equal to doing,
by himself alone, "what in France was the work
of an academy;" and that won for him the right
to mock, as Elijah the prophet mocked, for ever,
at the aid proffered by a man of the world when it
was no longer needed. But the perseverance that
yields not before frequent defeat, and repeated breaking of plan; and what often seems as mere blind
chance, or the sport of some malign power, demands
its special distinction, and, in this grand quality
of the spirit, CHARLES GORDON is in the very front
of our own common day of Pluto-worship and self-
centring activity. So. it was with "Miss Kate;"

her work was suddenly hindered, broken up, at one place and another—at Parkhurst, Shorncliffe, Woolwich, Faversham, C——, always from causes external to herself, yet on each occasion save the last (which *alone*, under accelerated physical weakness, never to cease, seemed to touch her very soul) she took up, in each new abode, the work which might there be done, heartily; and I think this unfaltering " doing as she had ever done " proved more than anything else the royal temper of her charity and life-action. It is truly a divine grace that will not be diverted, by any human accidents, from persevering in God's work. Many may be equal to a continued work that suffers no interruption, or breaking up; but it is human nature, after repeated interruptions, or breakings up and *losses*, to rebel against the sway of evil over good, and to *resent* it, like Achilles in his tent, or to throw up the hands in sorrow, and say, with the prophet, " It is enough. Now, O Lord, let me die, for I am not better than my fathers."

READING.—It might be thought that either the previous sketches are overcharged with records and references to incessant work, or that truth leaves no time for much reading to fill up the picture; but " Miss Kate " was always a *great* reader. Not a few of her friends were writers of books, but, beyond this circle, she read history—her own country's specially —with keen interest, and studied its characters so closely that often it seemed as if she had personal knowledge of them and their lives. The *Biographies* of great actors in the human life-drama were ever attractive in a high degree, the right vision of truth being her ceaseless aim and motive. Novels, too, were a furniture of her choice, and, in an inconceivably short interval, she would get through volume upon volume ; her rule being to catch the tone and characters of each, and, as good or bad, to cast aside or read again. To read over and again some book for refreshment or instruction has been commended from Horace downwards—

" Ter purè lecto poterunt recreare libello "—*Epp.*, lib. i.,

and " Miss Kate " often did this, unconsciously following many great names in the world, literary and others : perhaps in the floods of books now flowing from the press, the rush of modern life, and its infinite variety of subjects, there are few who will keep to the old way henceforth. In this way she had a fund of subjects for reflection, a gallery of figures, and stores of extracts ; whilst a very strong and accurate memory enabled her to pass before the eye, vividly, scenes and

situations, and touches of character, highly picturesque
and valued by me. Her reading of novels, however,
was not solely or chiefly for herself, but for others;
and, for advice and warning to young souls, she
made herself familiar with *their* modern-times' books.
Gradually she stored up a useful library of such light
reading, for lending to the circle in which she lived.
The sensational, the vile immoral, the babblers of
vice, seduction, murder, crime—books written merely
for the market—the low-toned, fibreless trash of the
book-stalls, were discarded; her desire being the
indulgence of young souls with literature, which they
will now have, but to keep away from them its moral
poison. Her condemnation of women authors—too
many even *young* women—writing in detail of foul
scenes and gross immoralities, any knowledge of
which carries shame, was almost a passion, softened
only by pity. Poetry was her choice, from pure love
of itself, and her memory was rich in extracts,
which, suddenly in quiet hours, she would repeat,
in a measured, soft and musical voice, for confirmation or illustration; and quaintly surprising were
many of these rare flowers, gathered in distant places
by the springs of other days, deserted now too much
for fashion's favourites.

With this slight reference to written lore may well

be named another trait for my Statue—her singular
and wide knowledge of proverbs, folk-lore, and West-
country sayings ; and her familiarity with phrase and
manner of the poor in their daily life—all the effect
of intense sympathy and life-long labours among
them and for them. Often and again some such
matter, striking me as new, would be claimed as
a life-long memory, with its particular surroundings ;
so that it was a pleasantry to retort " it's no use
telling you anything, your ' good people ' have told
you all."

COURAGE.—Many a proof of this might have been
added to that when, writing of the sea-storm, she said,
" I am no coward," and that about the child and the
bull.   An *amusing* one recurs here.   We had a marvellous breed of Persian cats some twenty years ago
—the pure blood of the royal present to the Queen
by the Shah—and one was a formidable fellow, stern
and terrific to trespassers on his dignity ; a great
brown giant.   He had one day been greatly guilty,
as " 'twas his nature to ;" but the question was who
should " bell the cat," when suddenly " Miss Kate "
appeared at the dining-room door, calmly walking
in, with the beast gripped by the neck with her firm
hand, and holding him at arm's length, whilst he, with

Great brown ' Elf,' a culprit.
From Editor's Pencil Sketch.

winking eyes, had all four paws curled up, and his huge "brush" hanging long and quivering, in most abject plight, and not attempting to move; to the vast amusement of the spectators! The strength required thus to hold such a weight at arm's length was an astonishment; but it was really will-force far more than physical—strength in weakness.

THE HELP-MEET.—The parson's wife is in English Church and social life a peculiar figure. Often, alas! a trial and no *meet* help to him, albeit not evil or different from other women; but just as she fails to realize and accept the conditions that, as he by his ordination is different from other men, so she must partake of his lot and responsibility, her peculiar mission is marred. It is, of course, possible to exaggerate this aspect of her life, and to do harm by "overdoing" it. Some wives are said to help their husbands with sermon writing, as laymen and statesmen are alleged to have had like help in their speeches and other ways; and, unless the truth must "give the world the lie," *great* statesmen have owed to their wives, in their public deliverances, more than may be openly acknowledged. "Miss Kate" was no such help-meet, nor was she a critic, or an applauder of sermons, or a reverent waiter and watcher, jealous of her hus

band's public performance and utterances. With
right and deep reverence for his holy office, into it
she never intruded in any way, save as a simple
helper in her own line. She hardly ever commented
upon his sermons; never was in raptures at others'
praise of this or that "fine" or "eloquent" discourse.
By tacit agreement we kept wholly apart my solemn
ministry from mere conversational comments. She
knew my dislike to such, and that my sole aim was
instruction, impression, and building up the Christian
life, with absolute renunciation therein of personal
ambition. Yet, if there were a point of humour, or
a "scene" concerned, she would tell it off to me
in a few words. Thus on one occasion an Eton
scholar, "Queen's Counsel," and well-known personality, was recreating in the county parish where I
was doing the work of the absent Vicar—a good
parish priest, and himself also an Eton man; and
"Miss Kate" had this little story for me: "You
would have been amused at Mrs. H——'s (the Q. C.'s
wife) account of the Vicar's visit to them (his stray
parishioners) on his return. She said, 'My husband
hardly had a word to say to him but about Mr.
Hobson's sermon on Good Friday: he so overflowed
with its fulness that he left no time to speak of
anything else.'" But again, if there were a mistake,

omission, defect of voice, or otherwise, that might be
the poor people's loss, the rule of silence was set by,
and a brief note was made of it and quietly told,
"You said so and so to-day;" "You omitted
a verse;" or "Your voice was quite low to-day. You
could scarcely be heard." Such "notes" are indeed
a parson's precious counsels. Often and often have
I known a poor brother, with some peculiarity of
voice, manner, or other defect, of which he was wholly
unconscious, which hindered his ministry and covered
greater excellencies; and yet, with a good and loving spouse — yea, with the addition of grown-up
children—he was never told of what he could not
see himself, though too patent to others. I remember such a defect to which my attention, as senior
chaplain, was called *officially* and peremptorily by
a great person, with an unwarranted demand of
actual *suspension of the offender from the pulpit!*
Whilst firmly declining this stern demand, I yet
named the defect to the offender kindly, only to
hear him say, to my surprise, that he (a most humble
man of not usual attainments), "though having little
else that he could do well yet, had always thought
that that (reading) was his *strong point!*" Neither
wife nor child had ever spoken to him of the
provoking and glaring fault. "Miss Kate" would

never have spared her rightful warning in such a case.

A more morbid development of the clerical marital relation is amusing. A vicar and his wife were devotedly attached to each other, with a large family; the wife advanced in the so-called Evangelical " Gospel;" the husband correct, conscientious, attentive to his parish in Sunday Church Services and week-day visitings; the Church Service was rigid, frigid, shivering under an idea of "dignity;" the *preaching* nowhere; but in its place, often, a neat address, lecture, or essay—written—such, in manner and form, as schoolmasters affect from the high desk. It was a queer couple, in modern life, this vicar and " vicaress." Save in actual ministrations in church, they were inseparable; they always walked arm-in-arm in the village street, and she accompanied him even in his ministerial visits to the sick poor. Their mutual bond of admiration was akin to that of a more ancient couple of men—

> " Frater erat Romæ Consulti Rhetor, ut alter
> Alterius sermone meros audiret honores
> Gracchus ut hic illi foret, huic ut Mucius ille."

He to her was as Solomon; she to him a very *Deborah*. Such simplicity was touching, but mis-

chievous; for his many ministerial visits were marred
in their very essence—the *private* presence of the
minister; and *her* interference was assumed and
known, to the reproach of *his* independence. There
was no limit to her devotion and admiration, or to
the sphere of her interference and voluble advice,
and no measure to the worship expected toward
him. Once, in a weak moment, I ventured to say,
" That was a nice little discourse to-day," but great
was my offence; for, in wrath and scorn, the "vicaress " replied, " A nice *little* discourse, indeed !"
with the addition of other sentiments; and so I
avoided that rock in future. Alas! for our subtle
human nature, deceiving and deceived: all unconsciously it was at work even here; *she* put him on
a high pedestal, admired and superior, and, finding
how to direct or control him, *she* felt uplifted to his
level of office, and " had her reward " in conscious
power and dignity; but, therefore, her responsibility
was terrible, when her influence reached even to
a question of clerical action on a moral and ecclesiastical matter. " Miss Kate," with all her courage
and life-long experience, would never have " dared "
to claim such a position. None could more regard
a husband's sacred office, but, therefore, she never
presumed to aim at being its director.

HOARDING !—An ominous word, but hallowed by its motive ! She requisitioned her drapers and my tailor, and from other sources, unknown to me, she had always a seemingly unlimited store of things safely kept; silk fragments, lace, ribbons, bits of chain, gold and silver fringes, borderings, relics, unimaginable accumulations of every sort; buttons of multitudinous variety; brooches, bracelets, pebbles, precious stones, crosses, jewellers' work, ornaments, coins, embroideries, and, in short, what not? Stowed away in all corners, cupboards, boxes, her stock never appeared to run out—a veritable "old curiosity shop" of varieties, only hidden away till called for. It was an old joke that she might have been a pirate's daughter, or a receiver of stolen goods. Whatever any one wanted she was thought always to have; and times innumerable some friend would mention some small want, or *I* might be at a loss for some matter, and the friend either had her desire at once, or a promise to "look out" for it, or my demand would be met by "Miss Kate's" silent disappearance, and return, bearing the treasure desired. These were her "things new and old," of which she made the rarest use.

LOVE OF CHILDREN.—It was no idle admiration

or passing enjoyment, but a settled, unfailing love, in the heart, which led her to be ever caring for them, in many ways. Her treasures were for them, boys and girls; and her labour to gratify them was great. The magical facility of finger was devoted to making children's robes, playthings, dolls. Often as many as fifty of the latter were her own contribution to sales for *The Orphanage*, dressed after newest fashions, or in quaintest costumes. All her treasures were needed and nothing was spared, and her " turn-outs " were an astonishment—the effect of life-long practice, like the priceless taste of a practised artist whose gift of touch no mere labour may compare with. Quiet days and tranquil hours had thus their register above, where " the cup of cold water " is not without its reward. It is a " thing of beauty " and " a joy for ever " to remember these ever-vanished scenes. With a book before her; her table covered with her handy hoards [b], she would stitch and stitch, in mere routine, whilst intent upon the action and contents of the volume under perusal, with careful examination. She had also a peculiarity with *poor*

[b] Our dining-table was for daily use very large, exhausting the air of the room, and my protest was useless, for she *must* have it so for her work's sake, specially for huge lengths of church texts, decorations, or arranging of material.

children; wherever she met them they were passed
with a gentle courtesy. She did not receive their curt-
seys or touch of the cap in a cold, dignity-style, or in
silence, but always—generally preceding them—with
a soft " good morning," or " good evening ;" and so
it was with poor people: they were not made to
feel their inferiority, but rather the grace that is due
from the higher life. Sundays were a special gift-
day. The choir changed their library-books at the
house, and carried away flowers or fruit, in their
season, and all year round some little memento,
book, picture, or other prize. No wonder that on
her burial seven of the old choir, after seven years'
separation, brought their floral cross, on that wild
wintry day, to see her laid in the peaceful church-
yard, and to make the service in church and at the
grave musically beautiful and soothing.

DISINTERESTEDNESS.—This feature has in a measure appeared through all *my* sketch, and from the
observations of others. Perfect disinterestedness is
rare and very hard to attain, for there are many
matters which the word *interest* may cover, besides
those where worldly profit, gain, or advantage, are
chief—·gratification of a desire; satisfaction of some
ideal; the accomplishment of some aim—all these,

when made the motive of action, being personal, are interested motives; and not seldom the real innermost motive is hidden from the actor's own thought. He or she has often a secret "reward," very precious though unconfessed—a sense of personal importance, a felt influence, some real if indirect power and—these are cherished attainments to many, though none have the vulgar meaning of self-interest. But perfect disinterestedness is free of every shadow of self, within and without, whether of material value, or of mere feeling. Fame, "the last infirmity of noble minds," has no privilege of exemption from selfishness; it is as a "fly in the ointment" of true disinterestedness; and yet deep, very deep, in Humanity's heart is the desire of fame in some form, and, if it be withheld from noble deeds and devoted action, it has power with many to embitter the memory and sadden the heart. There are those who, in all unconscious goodness, will toil and devote themselves to some good work without stint; who will willingly labour long "hoping for nothing again," but who, when the end has come and the occasion has passed, on looking back, will repine, not confessedly at the loss of direct "reward"—for that would reveal their personal motive—but upon the assumed high ground of the "injustice" or "ingratitude" of the world, in not awarding their deserved memorial crown. Alas! such simple souls, self-deceived, knew it not, but, secretly, through all their work, there lurked the worldly ideal, the thought of the world's praise, "the honour that cometh of men." They were not *satisfied* with the mere truth that *all* their works were "remembered before God," though the perfect self-surrender in every aspect, and the utter self-forgetfulness, in the present and in the future, which their work demanded, in order to be "perfect" might be absent. To this high but true ideal I fear not to claim that "Miss Kate" attained—or *grew*, for it was in the gift of grace to her nature, a simple outcome of her real life. She had an absolute indifference to all record of the past, for her own sake. She *could* not, I feel sure, have grieved at being "unacknowledged and almost unknown," or forgotten wholly. She was incapable of the faintest desire for any recognition; and knowing this so intimately as I do, and the utterness of her self-abnegation, I would not have written this sketch save under the dominance of a belief that the record may be of benefit to *others;* which hope alone would have gained *her* consent to it. The fact of such a life of self-obliteration may be strange, but it is possible and true. It is no doubt hard to conceive such a fact in the mass of characters around us, with their contrasted and opposite lines of action. The late Dean Stanley records, and without apology for such an effect, that his good sister Mary's life was "*shaded* by her public labours being from various causes unacknowledged and almost unknown." To one who had himself such gifts of worldly admiration, and was so prominent and protruding a figure in the world's eye, it might seem difficult to imagine another without a desire for "acknowledgment" or to be "known," but I would fain hope that Mary Stanley had no real shadow over her life as asserted, and that the Dean's "own feeling is reflected in what he says of his sister." Alas! and alas! how many well known examples there are of those who have endured "the cold *shade* of neglect" without repining—of unacknowledged goodness, labours, talents, devotion, in the Church's ministry, and everywhere — whose experience one would grieve to think had not its own high reward in the simple doing of—

"Just what they were *meant* to do,"

beyond which there was no desire or expectation. "I have loved righteousness and hated iniquity,

M

therefore I die in exile," is a sad memento of the world's neglect, but—

" 'Tis not so above,"

and the saints leave *their* record *there!*

CHEERFULNESS.—A grey or gloomy day is, in the outer world, not unlike a sombre or sad countenance and manner inside a house. Some people are as a "wet blanket" upon the enjoyableness of ordinary life; and for the most part such unfortunates cannot help it. Cheerfulness is not an acquired talent or quality; it runs in the veins of a sweet nature, like spontaneous music. There is no imitating it: the *effort* to be cheerful is rarely successful, and the hollow semblance of the artificial thing says—

" . . . . As plain as whisper in the ear
The place is haunted."

Cheerfulness is not easily to be described: it is something that is *felt*, and only realised by experience: it is not as *one* note, but as a harmony: it is the general effect of voice, look, manner, action, temper, temperament, spirit and—heart-ease! "A merry heart maketh a cheerful countenance." The possession of this gift is a valid treasure: it brightens

life and gives colour to its dull routine : it abides in
a house as a visible presence with a halo of peace,
and many a nameless sign. " Miss Kate " was gifted
with this " grace of life," and its perennial outflow
knew no change, save under the actual pressure of
acute suffering, when, for a time, the outward signs
were unseen, as stars behind a passing cloud. Physical suffering sometimes made her look very aged,
but the swift return to her natural *sheen* was always
near, and the change wondrous. Low spirits were
ever unknown to her—against her nature : the higher
life *ruled*, and her calm and even way, her lightened
and lightening personality, her trustful and restful
spirit of faith, stood aloof from and above the power
of real sadness ; nor was the gift for herself alone ;
it seemed hardly possible for saddened hearts to
remain so in her presence. She who called her[a]
"the bonniest bird of God" had rightly caught her
ideal trait, for she ever seemed silently uttering the
warning voice—

> " Low spirits are a sin ;"

and—

> " Hark ! hark ! the lark at Heaven's gate sings."

[a] Photograph facing p. 121.

·THE RECORD IS MADE ; my Statue is moulded ;
first by Hands invisible—to endure for ever; in
whose fashioning—

"Many a blow and biting sculpture
Polished well the stone elect,"

and now by my weak hands—to stand for a brief
day and then be forgotten.   It will be noted that
I have given no tracing directly of the inner life as
spiritual, nor was it easy to do this, if desirable ; the
hush, habitual, of her soul was, on secret spiritual
motions and emotion, so deep as to claim the truest
reverence ; albeit *I* knew and shared its silent power
—incapable, alas ! of *all*—and it seemed to me that
the simplest narrative would effectually show how
and where her spirit *rested*—by "the fresh springs "
of God—and wrought, so as to be made capable of
that life of unceasing labour and influence on other
souls—*si monumentum quæris circumspice*—for her
life-work was essentially spiritual ; such work would
only grow on a real spiritual root, and be sustained by
spiritual exercises and "the Communion of the Holy
Ghost ;" yet a scheme of daily living to this end ;
a direction of routine to be observed rigidly, if alway
observed, was ·observed so unobtrusively (just like
her still reserve of thought) as to escape observation,

beyond the "necessary things" of daily reading, meditation, work, and prayer. It is not possible, I often have felt, to make every spirit live by the same rule, any more than to make different physical constitutions thrive on the same food, or be cured by the same medicine ; one man's cure is another's bane ; and so it is largely with Spirits. Of the many manuals and directions for spiritual guidance—specially those of modern times, often written with seeming authority by names without power or large experience—the use is to little profit, and not seldom attended with disadvantage, their very ideal vitiated by the forgetfulness of the vast variety in souls, and of the innumerable ways in which God is pleased to nourish and shape them for Himself. A manual used as obligatory is, if imperfectly followed, a snare to tender consciences, "making those sad whom God has not made sad ;" or if rigidly adhered to may ensnare by being virtually itself made the measure of obligation, rather than the very spiritual things to which it should refer all finality ; and so, its "cut and dried" rules being scrupulously kept, it becomes a temptation to spiritual confidence, or assurance without interior warrant. But, though I care not to give details, I may be pardoned for saying that no one could have lived with " Miss Kate "

daily without becoming conscious of a spiritual force
and presence in and around her ; yea, so patent was
this, in her habitually sustained ways, that one came
to feel a certain feeling of *safety* in her presence, as
of one "under the shadow of the Almighty;" and
surely never was there given to me to see a soul
more unchangeably and vitally *set* upon God in
Christ than hers, which is now with His saints in
paradise.

HER BOOKS.—"Reading makes a full man," but
Johnson, I think, pronounced one of his verdicts
that a man with a large library need not be feared :
though that is only a half-truth, the grain of fact
being, probably, that few such men read all the
books they have. It is a larger truth that any one's
choice books—his friends and companions—show the
tone and character of his or her mental and spiritual
life. My "Miss Kate's" general reading has been
mentioned as large and habitual; her *chosen* books
were significant. From early days she had always
about her, "The Holy Oblation;" "Breviary" and
"The Hours;" "The Cathedral;" "Taylor's Holy
Living and Dying;" "Thoughts in Past Years;"
"The Divine Master;" "Days and Seasons;" "Verses
for Holy Seasons;" "George Herbert." Added in

after days were "Thomas à Kempis;" "The Christian Year;" "Hymns and Poems for the Sick and Suffering;" "Disce Vivere;" "Proctor's Legends and
Lyrics;" "Eucharistica;" "Thoughts on Personal
Religion;" "The Holy Catholic Church." One or
two, obviously, need not be added here—her small
book of the Psalms, Bible, Prayer-Book, &c. The
last-named is noticeable as having pasted on to its
first blank leaf an extract from Beveridge which we
have much used. It was first printed by her sister
(Mrs. Autridge), and used far and wide.

"AN EXPERIMENT."

"Let any one that hath a due sense of religion, and
a real desire of happiness, let such a one make trial of our
Church but for one year, let him constantly read the Scriptures
in the method that she prescribes, let him constantly use the
"Common Prayer" according to her directions, let him constantly observe all her fasts and holy-days, let him receive the
Sacrament as often as she is ready to administer it, and perform
whatsoever else she hath been pleased to command,—let any
man, I say, do this, and then let him be against our Church if
he can. I am confident he cannot. But our misery is, that
none of those that are out of the Church, and but few of those
who are in it, will make the experiment, and this is the reason
that those are so violent against her, and these so indifferent to
her."—*Bp. Beveridge.*

Many of her books have passages carefully noted,
or marked. This is from "The Divine Master:"—

" Master, I bow me down in shame and confusion of face, to think that I should have dared to doubt, that what Thou didst command would be made possible even unto me; it is enough, *I go to seek Thee, where the desolate and poor, in soul and body, shall give me the unutterable joy of tending Thee.*"

This one marking is selected merely as showing indirectly her great life-purpose.

I may add " The Golden Grove " (1855), inscribed " In Remembrance of E. A." It was a gift from her friend, the other " Miss Anderson," on her leaving the Crimea sick in 1855, and has numerous gems of pencil sketches at sea and elsewhere, with markings throughout of passages specially valued, all, I believe, by the dear Donor. It may not be unmeet to give here a copy of an " In Memoriam " on Miss Emily Anderson's death in 1870 (from "*John Bull*") :—

" As one who daily labours on
　With some high Aim afar before,
And only rests when, Daylight gone,
　The time for working is no more ;

So daily, in her chosen way,
　She toiled the Calling high to gain ;
And only rests when Life's closed day
　Frees her from earthly grief and pain.

She rests as only one may rest,
  In blessedness of Hope and Peace,
Who all day wrought, by Love possessed,
  Where suffering wailed for near release ;

Her life-long work, her Lord's own poor
  To guide, to feed, to nurse and bless ;
To watch and haste where need was sure ;
  To sweeten aye Life's bitterness.

Such was her choice ! she, gentle born,
  Sought our rude Soldiers' wretched bed,
And soothed the frame by anguish worn
  In far-off lands, by pity led.

She, not the least where many shone
  (A noble Band of women weak),
Now to her sure reward is gone,
  To wear her Crown, holy and meek !

So one by one, like stars, they set ;
  The good, the gentle, loving, pure ;
Unseen awhile on earth and yet
  To rise with Christ in Glory sure.

O Lord we bless Thy sainted dead ;
  Help us like them to walk with Thee ;
In Faith and Hope and Love still led
  Till we with them shall perfect be."

The friends, severed in the flesh, after like labours have now again met for ever !

My own " Miss Kate " needs but one word more. If labours incessant and singularly attractive to loyal and devout Church servants ; if wide and ever-widen-

ing influence in varied spheres of action ; if utter de-
devotion and self-forgetting charity ; if an example of
actual common life, imitable, if not by all attainable,
spending and being spent under highest motives ; if
the giving of consolation to suffering, and sorrow, and
gladness to young souls ; if all this be not unworthy
of a brief record, and specially when all was the outcome of a *character* wondrously fashioned by " the
heavenly Architect," for the Master's use ; and all
wrought under the burthen of acute and complicated
suffering for thirty years and more ; then I have not
judged amiss in making, with feeble hand and bruised
heart, this brief and simple record of the truth, de-
siring only, and ascribing to God solely, who " hath
wrought all our works in us," all blessing, thanks-
giving, and praise for His supernatural work of grace,
in one human Soul now—

> " Gone out of sight ! to that well-studied shore
>   Where thou hadst thought to anchor many a year ;
> Like a full shock ripe for the harvest store,
>   A wakeful watcher when thy Lord drew near.
>
> Like one who steadfast through the changeful night,
>   Watching the star-ways and the constant pole,
> Has steered aright by Heaven's unchanging light,
>   And gains his port as back the shadows roll."

The Sultan's Brooch.
In profile, the centre of jewelled Enamel—an Eastern Dome in shape—
stands out nearly a half-globe.

THE SULTAN'S BROOCH.

FOR many years the brooch was not worn, but, after frequent requests to see it, "Miss Kate" was persuaded to wear it, and did so until she ceased to use her ordinary dress. At the last it was, with her wedding-ring and guard, put upon a violet velvet ribbon and hung round my neck, by her good maid, whilst I lay only half-conscious.

It is a remarkable ornament; unobtrusive but rich with enamel and diamonds; the crescent moon and star being set in the imperial colours. The gold setting is bold with simplicity.

Inscription.

"Presented by H.I.M. the Sultan TO MISS K. ANDERSON in acknowledgment OF HER SERVICES IN THE HOSPITALS OF THE BRITISH ARMY in the East, 1856."

The reader of this sketch now knows what solemn memories clustered round that simple thing—unknown for many years to others, who saw in it only a costly ornament.

NOTE TO p. 47.

WHEN writing this page, the late Dean Stanley's remarks about his sister Mary's "public labours" being "without acknowledgment and for the most part unknown" were not before me. After referring to his book ("Memoirs of Edward and Catharine Stanley") I have spoken of this case in another aspect later on (p. 161), but here I would record the case as an illustration of the remarks on the former page. Among the "causes," referred to but not named by the Dean, for the supposed neglect of his sister, was mainly the overshadowing of Miss Nightingale's representative name, which, however, equally affected *all* the Lady-nurses, but, I hope, without "casting a shade over their lives."

Printed by Parker and Co., Crown Yard, Oxford.

A SELECTION FROM THE PUBLICATIONS OF
PARKER AND CO.
OXFORD, AND 6 SOUTHAMPTON-STREET,
STRAND, LONDON.

The Seven Sayings from the Cross :
ADDRESSES by WILLIAM BRIGHT, D.D., Canon of Christ
Church, Oxford. Fcap. 8vo., limp cloth, 1s. 6d.

Lays of the Early English Church.
By W. FOXLEY NORRIS, M.A., Rector of Witney. Fcap. 8vo.,
cloth, with Twelve Illustrations, 3s. 6d.

The Church in England from William III.
to Victoria.
By the Rev. A. H. HORE, M.A., Trinity College, Oxford.
2 vols., Post 8vo., cloth, 15s.

The Philosophy of Church-Life,
Or The Church of Christ viewed as the Means whereby God
manifests Himself to Mankind. By the late RICHARD TUDOR,
B.A., Vicar of Swallowcliffe, Wilts; Author of "The Deca-
logue viewed as the Christian's Law," &c. 2 vols., 8vo.,
cloth, 16s.
" A work which we do not hesitate to pronounce one of the most important contributions to scientific theology that has been made in our
time."—John Bull.

In Memoriam.
SERMONS Preached on various Occasions (1861—1887), by
the late HENRY LINTON, M.A., Honorary Canon of Christ
Church, late Rector of St. Peter-le-Bailey, and formerly Fellow
of Magdalen College, Oxford. With an Introductory Sketch
of the Author, by the Rev. F. BOURDILLON, M.A., Vicar of
Old Warden. Crown 8vo., with Portrait of Canon Linton,
cloth, 5s.   [Just published.

St. Cyril on the Mysteries.
The Five Lectures of St. Cyril on the Mysteries, and other
Sacramental Treatises ; with Translations. Edited by the
Rev. H. DE ROMESTIN, M.A., Great Maplestead, Essex.
Fcap. 8vo., cloth, 3s.   [See also p. 3.

Διδαχὴ τῶν δώδεκα Ἀποστόλων.
THE TEACHING OF THE TWELVE APOSTLES.
The Greek Text with English Translation, Introduction,
Notes, and Illustrative Passages. By the Rev. H. DE RO-
MESTIN, Incumbent of Freeland, and Rural Dean. Second
Edition. Fcap. 8vo., cloth, 3s.   [See also p. 3.

On Faith and the Creed :
Dogmatic Teaching of the Church of the Fourth and Fifth
Centuries : being a Translation of the several Treatises con-
tained in the Compilation entitled De Fide et Symbolo :
by the Rev. CHARLES A. HEURTLEY, D.D., Margaret Professor of Divinity, and Canon of Ch. Ch., Oxford. Second
Edition. Crown 8vo., cloth, 4s. 6d.   [See also p. 3.

[988.3*.50]

The Bampton Lectures for 1881.

THE ONE RELIGION : Truth, Holiness, and Peace desired by the Nations, and Revealed by Jesus Christ. By the Right Rev. the LORD BISHOP OF SALISBURY. Second Edition. Crown 8vo., cloth, 7s. 6d.

An Explanation of the Thirty-Nine Articles.

By the late A. P. FORBES, D.C.L., Bishop of Brechin. With an Epistle Dedicatory to the Rev. E. B. PUSEY, D.D. New Edition, in one vol., Post 8vo., 12s.

A Short Explanation of the Nicene Creed,

For the Use of Persons beginning the Study of Theology. By the late A. P. FORBES, D.C.L., Bishop of Brechin. New Edition, Crown 8vo., cloth, 6s.

The Apostles' Creed.

The Greek Origin of the Apostles' Creed Illustrated by Ancient Documents and Recent Research. By Rev. JOHN BARON, D.D., F.S.A. 8vo., cloth, with Seven Illustrations, 10s. 6d.

The Sacraments.

RICHARD BAXTER ON THE SACRAMENTS : Holy Orders, Holy Baptism, Confirmation, Absolution, Holy Communion. 18mo., cloth, 1s.

The History of Confirmation.

By WILLIAM JACKSON, M.A., Queen's College, Oxford ; Vicar of Heathfield, Sussex. Crown 8vo., cloth, 2s. 6d.

A Summary of the Ecclesiastical Courts Commission's Report:

And of Dr. STUBBS' Historical Reports ; together with a Review of the Evidence before the Commission. By SPENCER L. HOLLAND, Barrister-at-Law. Post 8vo., cloth, 7s. 6d.

A History of Canon Law

In conjunction with other Branches of Jurisprudence : with Chapters on the Royal Supremacy and the Report of the Commission on Ecclesiastical Courts. By Rev. J. DODD, M.A., formerly Rector of Hampton Poyle, Oxon. 8vo., cloth, 7s. 6d.

On Instructing the Unlearned.

SAINT AUGUSTINE, on Instructing the Unlearned, concerning Faith of Things not Seen, on the Advantage of Believing, the Enchiridion to Laurentius, or concerning Faith, Hope, and Charity. Edited by Rev. H. DE ROMESTIN, M.A., Vicar of Stony Stratford. Fcap. 8vo., cloth, 3s. 6d.   [See also p. 3.

On Eucharistical Adoration.

With Considerations suggested by a Pastoral Letter on the Doctrine of the Most Holy Eucharist. By the late Rev. JOHN KEBLE, M.A., Vicar of Hursley. 24mo., sewed, 2s.

The Catholic Doctrine of the Sacrifice and Participation of the Holy Eucharist.

By GEORGE TREVOR, M.A., D.D., Canon of York; Rector of Beeford. Second Edition. 8vo., cloth, 10s. 6d.

The Administration of the Holy Spirit. •

IN THE BODY OF CHRIST. The Bampton Lectures for 1868. By the late LORD BISHOP OF SALISBURY. Third Edition. Crown 8vo., 7s. 6d.

S. Athanasius on the Incarnation, &c.

S. Patris Nostri S. Athanasii Archiepiscopi Alexandriæ de Incarnatione Verbi, ejusque Corporali ad nos Adventu. With an English Translation by the Rev. J. RIDGWAY, B.D., Hon. Canon of Ch. Ch. Fcap. 8vo., cloth, 5s.

De Fide et Symbolo:

Documenta quædam nec non Aliquorum SS. Patrum Tractatus. Edidit CAROLUS A. HEURTLEY, S.T.P., Dom. Margaretæ Prælector, et Ædis Christi Canonicus. Editio Quarta, Recognita et Aucta. Crown 8vo., cloth, 4s. 6d.

Translation of the above.

Cloth, 4s. 6d. [See p. 1.

The Canons of the Church.

The Definitions of the Catholic Faith and Canons of Discipline of the First Four General Councils of the Universal Church. In Greek and English. Fcap. 8vo., cloth, 2s. 6d.

The English Canons.

The Constitutions and Canons Ecclesiastical of the Church of England, referred to their Original Sources, and Illustrated with Explanatory Notes, by MACKENZIE E. C. WALCOTT, B.D., F.S.A., Præcentor and Prebendary of Chichester. Fcap. 8vo., cloth, 2s. 6d.

Our Deus Homo.

Or Why God was made Man: by ST. ANSELM. Latin and English.

S. Aurelius Augustinus,

EPISCOPUS HIPPONENSIS,

De Catechizandis Rudibus, de Fide Rerum quæ non videntur, de Utilitate Credendi. A New Edition, with the Enchiridion. Fcap. 8vo., cloth, 3s. 6d.

Translation of the above.

Cloth, 3s. 6d. [See p. 2.

Vincentius Lirinensis

For the Antiquity and Universality of the Catholic Faith against the Profane Novelties of all Heretics. *Latin and English.* New Edition, Fcap. 8vo., 3s.

The Pastoral Rule of S. Gregory.

Sancti Gregorii Papæ Regulæ Pastoralis Liber, ad JOHANNEM, Episcopum Civitatis Ravennæ. With an English Translation. By the Rev. H. R. BRAMLEY, M.A., Fellow of Magdalen College, Oxford. Fcap. 8vo., cloth, 6s.

The Book of Ratramn.

The Priest and Monk of Corbey commonly called Bertram, on the Body and Blood of the Lord. (Latin and English.) Fcap. 8vo.

The Athanasian Creed.

A Critical History of the Athanasian Creed, by the Rev. DANIEL WATERLAND, D.D. Fcap. 8vo., cloth, 5s.

The "Didache."

See p. 1.

St. Cyril on the Mysteries.

See p. 1.

Studia Sacra :

Commentaries on the Introductory Verses of St. John's Gospel, and on a Portion of St. Paul's Epistle to the Romans; with an Analysis of St. Paul's Epistles, &c., by the late Rev. JOHN KEBLE, M.A.   8vo., cloth, 10s. 6d.

Discourses on Prophecy.

In which are considered its Structure, Use and Inspiration. By JOHN DAVISON, B.D.   Sixth and Cheaper Edition.   8vo., cloth, 9s.

The Worship of the Old Covenant

CONSIDERED MORE ESPECIALLY IN RELATION TO THAT OF THE New.   By the Rev. E. F. WILLIS, M.A., late Vice-Principal of Cuddesdon College.   Post 8vo., cloth, 5s.

A Summary of the Evidences for the Bible.

By the Rev. T. S. ACKLAND, M.A., late Fellow of Clare Hall, Cambridge ; Incumbent of Pollington cum Balne, Yorkshire. 24mo., cloth, 3s.

A Plain Commentary on the Book of Psalms

(Prayer-book Version), chiefly grounded on the Fathers.   For the Use of Families.   2 vols., Fcap. 8vo., cloth, 10s. 6d.

The Psalter and the Gospel.

The Life, Sufferings, and Triumph of our Blessed Lord, revealed in the Book of Psalms.   Fcap. 8vo., cloth, 2s.

The Study of the New Testament :

Its Present Position, and some of its Problems.   AN INAU-GURAL LECTURE delivered on Feb. 20th and 22nd, 1883. By W. SANDAY, M.A., D.D., Dean Ireland's Professor of the Exegesis of Holy Scripture.   64 pp. 8vo., in wrapper, 2s.

Sayings Ascribed to Our Lord

By the Fathers and other Primitive Writers, and Incidents in His Life narrated by them, otherwise than found in Scrip-ture.   By JOHN THEODORE DODD, B.A., late Student of Christ Church, Oxford.   Fcap. 8vo., cloth, 3s.

A Commentary on the Epistles and Gospels in the Book of Common Prayer.

Extracted from Writings of the Fathers of the Holy Catholic Church, anterior to the Division of the East and West.   With an Introductory Notice by the DEAN OF ST. PAUL'S.   2 vols., Crown 8vo., cloth, 10s. 6d.

Catena Aurea.

A Commentary on the Four Gospels, collected out of the Works of the Fathers by S. THOMAS AQUINAS. Uniform with the Library of the Fathers. A Re-issue, complete in 6 vols., cloth, £2 2s.

A Plain Commentary on the Four Holy Gospels,

Intended chiefly for Devotional Reading. By the Very Rev. J. W. BURGON, B.D., Dean of Chichester. New Edition. 4 vols., Fcap. 8vo., limp cloth, £1 1s.

The Last Twelve Verses of the Gospel according to S. Mark

Vindicated against Recent Critical Objectors and Established, by the Very Rev. J. W. BURGON, B.D., Dean of Chichester. With Facsimiles of Codex ℵ and Codex L. 8vo., cloth, 6s.

The Gospels from a Rabbinical Point of View,

Shewing the perfect Harmony of the Four Evangelists on the subject of our Lord's Last Supper, and the Bearing of the Laws and Customs of the Jews at the time of our Lord's coming on the Language of the Gospels. By the Rev. G. WILDON PIERITZ, M.A. Crown 8vo., limp cloth, 3s.

Christianity as Taught by S. Paul.

By WILLIAM J. IRONS, D.D., of Queen's College, Oxford; Prebendary of S. Paul's; being the BAMPTON LECTURES for the Year 1870, with an Appendix of the CONTINUOUS SENSE of S. Paul's Epistles; with Notes and Metalegomena, 8vo., with Map, Second Edition, with New Preface, cloth, 9s.

S. Paul's Epistles to the Ephesians and Philippians.

A Practical and Exegetical Commentary. Edited by the late Rev. HENRY NEWLAND. 8vo., cloth, 7s. 6d.

The Explanation of the Apocalypse.

By VENERABLE BEDA, Translated by the Rev. EDW. MARSHALL, M.A., F.S.A., formerly Fellow of Corpus Christi College, Oxford. 180 pp. Fcap. 8vo., cloth, 3s. 6d.

A History of the Church,

From the Edict of Milan, A.D. 313, to the Council of Chalcedon, A.D. 451. By WILLIAM BRIGHT, D.D., Regius Professor of Ecclesiastical History, and Canon of Christ Church, Oxford. Second Edition. Post 8vo., 10s. 6d.

The Age of the Martyrs;

Or, The First Three Centuries of the Work of the Church of our Lord and Saviour Jesus Christ. By the late JOHN DAVID JENKINS, B.D., Fellow of Jesus College, Oxford ; Canon of Pieter Maritzburg. Cr. 8vo., cl., reduced to 3s. 6d.

Eighteen Centuries of the Church in England.

By the Rev. A. H. HORE, M.A. Trinity College, Oxford. 712 pp. Demy 8vo., cloth, 15s.

The Ecclesiastical History of the First Three Centuries,

From the Crucifixion of Jesus Christ to the year 313. By the late Rev. Dr. BURTON. Fourth Edition. 8vo., cloth, 12s.

A Brief History of the Christian Church,

From the First Century to the Reformation. By the Rev. J. S. BARTLETT. Fcap. 8vo., cloth, 2s. 6d.

A History of the English Church,

From its Foundation to the Reign of Queen Mary. By MARY CHARLOTTE STAPLEY. Fourth Edition, revised, with a Recommendatory Notice by DEAN HOOK. Crown 8vo., cloth, 5s.

Bede's Ecclesiastical History of the English Nation.

A New Translation by the Rev. L. GIDLEY, M.A., Chaplain of St. Nicholas', Salisbury. Crown 8vo., cloth, 6s.

· St. Paul in Britain ;

Or, The Origin of British as opposed to Papal Christianity. By the Rev. R. W. MORGAN. Second Edition. Crown 8vo., cloth, 2s. 6d.

The Sufferings of the Clergy during the Great Rebellion.

By the Rev. JOHN WALKER, M.A., sometime of Exeter College, Oxford, and Rector of St. Mary Major, Exeter. Epitomised by the Author of "The Annals of England." Second Edition. Fcap. 8vo., cloth, 2s. 6d.

Missale ad usum Insignis et Præclaræ Ecclesiæ Sarum.

Ed. F. H. DICKINSON, A.M. Complete in One Vol., 8vo., cl., 26s. Part II., 6s.; Part III., 10s. 6d.; and Part IV., 7s. 6d.; may still be had.

The First Prayer-book of Edward VI. Compared

With the Successive Revisions of the Book of Common Prayer. Together with a Concordance and Index to the Rubrics in the several Editions. Second Edition. Crown 8vo., cloth, 12s.

An Introduction

TO THE HISTORY OF THE SUCCESSIVE REVI-sions of the Book of Common Prayer. By JAMES PARKER, Hon. M.A. Oxon. Crown 8vo., pp. xxxii., 532, cloth, 12s.

The Principles of Divine Service;

Or, An Inquiry concerning the True Manner of Understand-ing and Using the Order for Morning and Evening Prayer, and for the Administration of the Holy Communion in the English Church. By the late Ven. PHILIP FREEMAN, M.A., Archdeacon of Exeter, &c. 2 vols., 8vo., cloth, 16s.

A History of the Book of Common Prayer,

And other Authorized Books, from the Reformation; with an Account of the State of Religion in England from 1640 to 1660. By the Rev. THOMAS LATHBURY, M.A. Second Edition, with an Index. 8vo., cloth, 5s.

The Prayer-Book Calendar.

THE CALENDAR OF THE PRAYER-BOOK ILLUS-TRATED. (Comprising the first portion of the "Calendar of the Anglican Church," with additional Illustrations, an Appendix on Emblems, &c.) With 200 Engravings from Me-dieval Works of Art. Sixth Thousand. Fcap. 8vo., cl., 6s.

A CHEAP EDITION OF

The First Prayer-Book

As issued by the Authority of the Parliament of the Second Year of King Edward VI. 1549. Eighth Thousand. 24mo., limp cloth, price 1s.

Also,

The Second Prayer-Book of Edward VI.

Issued 1552. Fourth Thousand. 24mo., limp cloth, price 1s.

Ritual Conformity.

Interpretations of the Rubrics of the Prayer-Book, agreed upon by a Conference held at All Saints, Margaret-street, 1880—1881. Third Edition, 80 pp. Crown 8vo., in wrapper, 1s.

The Ornaments Rubrick,

ITS HISTORY AND MEANING. Fourth Thousand. 72 pp., Crown 8vo., 6d.

The Catechist's Manual;

By EDW. M. HOLMES, Rector of Marsh Gibbon, Bicester. With an Introduction by the late SAMUEL WILBERFORCE, LORD BP. OF WINCHESTER. 6th Thousand. Cr. 8vo., limp cl., 5s.

The Confirmation Class-book:

Notes for Lessons, with APPENDIX, containing Questions and Summaries for the Use of the Candidates. By EDWARD M. HOLMES, LL.B.', Author of the "Catechist's Manual." Second Edition, Fcap. 8vo., limp cloth, 2s. 6d.

> THE QUESTIONS, separate, 4 sets, in wrapper, 1s.
> THE SUMMARIES, separate, 4 sets, in wrapper, 1s.

Catechetical Lessons on the Book of Common Prayer.

Illustrating the Prayer-book, from its Title-page to the end of the Collects, Epistles, and Gospels. Designed to aid the Clergy in Public Catechising. By the Rev. Dr. FRANCIS HESSEY, Incumbent of St. Barnabas, Kensington. Fcap. 8vo., cloth, 6s.

Catechising Notes on the Apostles' Creed;

The Ten Commandments; The Lord's Prayer; The Confirmation Service; The Forms of Prayer at Sea, &c. By A WORCESTERSHIRE CURATE. Crown 8vo., in wrapper, 1s.

The Church's Work in our Large Towns.

By GEORGE HUNTINGTON, M.A., Rector of Tenby, and Domestic Chaplain of the Rt. Hon. the Earl of Crawford and Balcarres. Second Edit., revised and enlarged. Cr. 8vo., cl. 3s. 6d.

Notes of Seven Years' Work in a Country Parish.

By R. F. WILSON, M.A., Prebendary of Sarum, and Examining Chaplain to the Bishop of Salisbury. Fcap. 8vo., cloth, 4s.

A Manual of Pastoral Visitation,

Intended for the Use of the Clergy in their Visitation of the Sick and Afflicted. By A PARISH PRIEST. Dedicated, by permission, to His Grace the Archbishop of Dublin. Second Edition, Crown 8vo., limp cloth, 3s. 6d. ; roan, 4s.

The Cure of Souls.

By the Rev. G. ARDEN, M.A., Rector of Winterborne-Came, and Author of "Breviates from Holy Scripture," &c. Fcap. 8vo., cloth, 2s. 6d.

Questions on the Collects, Epistles, and Gospels,

Throughout the Year. Edited by the Rev. T. L. CLAUGHTON, Vicar of Kidderminster. For the Use of Teachers in Sunday Schools. Fifth Edition, 18mo., cl. In two Parts, each 2s. 6d.

Addresses to the Candidates for Ordination on the Questions in the Ordination Service.

By the late SAMUEL WILBERFORCE, LORD BISHOP OF WINCHESTER. Fifth Thousand. Crown 8vo., cloth, 6s.

Tracts for the Christian Seasons.

FIRST SERIES. Edited by JOHN ARMSTRONG, D.D., late Lord Bishop of Grahamstown. 4 vols. complete, Fcap. 8vo., cloth, 12s.

SECOND SERIES. Edited by JOHN ARMSTRONG, D.D., late Lord Bishop of Grahamstown. 4 vols. complete, Fcap. 8vo., cloth, 10s.

THIRD SERIES. Edited by JAMES RUSSELL WOODFORD, D.D., late Lord Bishop of Ely. 4 vols., Fcap. 8vo., cloth, 14s.

Faber's Stories from the Old Testament.

With Four Illustrations. New Edition. Square Crown 8vo., cloth, 4s.

Holy Order.

A CATECHISM. By CHARLES S. GRUEBER, Vicar of S. James, Hambridge, Diocese of Bath and Wells. 220 pp. 24mo., in wrapper, 3s.

By the same Author.

The Church of England the Ancient Church of the Land.

Its Property. Disestablishment and Disendowment. Fate of Sacrilege. Work and Progress of the Church, &c., &c. A CATECHISM. Second Edition, 24mo., in wrapper, 1s.

A Catechism on the Kingdom of God:

For the Use of the Children of the Kingdom in Sunday and Day Schools. Second Edition, 70 pp. 24mo., cloth, 1s.; in stiff wrapper, 6d.

"Is Christ Divided?"

On Unity in Religion, and the Sin and Scandal of Schism, That is to say, of Division, Disunion, Separation, among Christians. A CATECHISM. 8vo., in wrapper, 1s.

The Catechism of the Church of England

Commented upon, and Illustrated from the Holy Scriptures and the Book of Common Prayer, with Appendices on Confirmation, &c., &c. 24mo., limp cloth, 1s.; cloth boards, 1s. 6d.

For a Series of Parochial Books and Tracts published by Messrs. Parker, see the Parochial Catalogue.

Oxford Editions of Devotional Works.

Fcap. 8vo., chiefly printed in Red and Black, on Toned Paper.

Andrewes' Devotions.

DEVOTIONS. By the Right Rev. LANCELOT ANDREWES. Translated from the Greek and Latin, and arranged anew. Cloth, 5s.

The Imitation of Christ.

FOUR BOOKS. By THOMAS A KEMPIS. A new Edition, revised. Cloth, 4s.

Pocket Edition. 32mo., cloth, 1s.; bound, 1s. 6d.

Laud's Devotions.

THE PRIVATE DEVOTIONS of Dr. WILLIAM LAUD, Archbishop of Canterbury, and Martyr. Antique cloth, 5s.

Spinckes' Devotions.

TRUE CHURCH OF ENGLAND MAN'S COMPANION IN THE CLOSET. By NATHANIEL SPINCKES. Floriated borders, antique cloth, 4s.

Sutton's Meditations.

GODLY MEDITATIONS UPON THE MOST HOLY SACRAMENT OF THE LORD'S SUPPER. By CHRISTOPHER SUTTON, D.D., late Prebend of Westminster. A new Edition. Antique cloth, 5s.

Taylor's Golden Grove.

THE GOLDEN GROVE: A Choice Manual, containing what is to be Believed, Practised, and Desired or Prayed for. By BISHOP JEREMY TAYLOR. Antique cloth, 3s. 6d.

Taylor's Holy Living.

THE RULE AND EXERCISES OF HOLY LIVING. By BISHOP JEREMY TAYLOR. Antique cloth, 4s.

Pocket Edition. 32mo., cloth, 1s.; bound, 1s. 6d.

Taylor's Holy Dying.

THE RULE AND EXERCISES OF HOLY DYING. By BISHOP JEREMY TAYLOR. Ant. cloth, 4s.

Pocket Edition. 32mo., cloth, 1s.; bound, 1s. 6d.

Ancient Collects.

ANCIENT COLLECTS AND OTHER PRAYERS, Selected for Devotional Use from various Rituals, with an Appendix on the Collects in the Prayer-book. By WILLIAM BRIGHT, D.D. Fourth Edition. Antique cloth, 5s.

Devout Communicant.

THE DEVOUT COMMUNICANT, exemplified in his Behaviour before, at, and after the Sacrament of the Lord's Supper: Practically suited to all the Parts of that Solemn Ordinance. 7th Edition, revised. Edited by Rev. G. MOULTRIE. Fcap. 8vo., toned paper, red lines, ant. cloth, 4s.

ΕΙΚΩΝ ΒΑΣΙΛΙΚΗ.

THE PORTRAITURE OF HIS SACRED MAJESTY KING CHARLES I. in his Solitudes and Sufferings. New Edition, with an Historical Preface by C. M. PHILLIMORE. Cloth, 5s.

EUCHARISTICA:

Meditations and Prayers on the Most Holy Eucharist, from Old English Divines. With an Introduction by SAMUEL, LORD BISHOP OF OXFORD. A New Edition, revised by the Rev. H. E. CLAYTON, Vicar of S. Mary Magdalene, Oxford. In Red and Black, 32mo., cloth, 2s. 6d.—Cheap Edition, 1s.

DAILY STEPS TOWARDS HEAVEN ;

Or, PRACTICAL THOUGHTS on the GOSPEL HISTORY, for Every Day in the Year. Fiftieth Thousand. 32mo., roan, 2s. 6d. ; morocco, 5s.

LARGE-TYPE EDITION. Crown 8vo., cloth antique, 5s.

THE HOURS:

Being Prayers for the Third, Sixth, and Ninth Hours; with a Preface and Heads of Devotion for the Day. Seventh Edition. 32mo., 1s.

PRIVATE PRAYERS FOR A WEEK.

Compiled by WILLIAM BRIGHT, D.D., Canon of Christ Church, Oxford. 96 pp. Fcap. 8vo., limp cloth, 1s. 6d.

By the same Author.

FAMILY PRAYERS FOR A WEEK.

Fcap. 8vo., cloth, 1s.

STRAY THOUGHTS:

For Every Day in the Year. Collected and Arranged by E. L. 32mo., cloth, gilt, red edges, 1s.

OUTLINES OF INSTRUCTIONS

Or Meditations for the Church's Seasons. By JOHN KEBLE, M.A. Edited, with a Preface, by R. F. WILSON, M.A. Second Edition. Crown 8vo., cloth, toned paper, 5s.

SPIRITUAL COUNSEL, &C.

By the late Rev. J. KEBLE, M.A. Edited by R. F. WILSON, M.A. Fifth Edition. Post 8vo., cloth, 3s. 6d.

MEDITATIONS FOR THE FORTY DAYS OF LENT.

By the Author of "Charles Lowder." With a Prefatory Notice by the ARCHBISHOP OF DUBLIN. 18mo., cloth, 2s. 6d.

OF THE IMITATION OF CHRIST.

Four Books. By THOMAS A KEMPIS. Small 4to., printed on thick toned paper, with red border-lines, &c. Cloth, 12s.

PRAYERS FOR MARRIED PERSONS.

From Various Sources, chiefly from the Ancient Liturgies. Selected by C. WARD, M.A. Third Edition, Revised. 24mo., cloth, 4s. 6d. ; Cheap Edition, 2s. 6d.

FOR THE LORD'S SUPPER.

DEVOTIONS BEFORE AND AFTER HOLY COMMUNION. With Preface by J. KEBLE. Sixth Edition. 32mo., cloth, 2s. With the Office, cloth, 2s. 6d.

The late Osborne Gordon.

OSBORNE GORDON. A Memoir: with a Selection of his Writings. Edited by Geo. Marshall, M.A., Rector of Milton, Berks, &c. With Medallion Portrait, 8vo., cloth, 10s. 6d.

Dr. Preston.

THE LIFE OF THE RENOWNED DR. PRESTON. Writ by his Pupil, Master Thomas Ball, D.D., Minister of Northampton in the year 1628. Edited by E. W. Harcourt, Esq., M.P. Crown 8vo., cloth, 4s.

Rev. John Keble.

A MEMOIR OF THE REV. JOHN KEBLE, M.A., late Vicar of Hursley. By the Right Hon. Sir J. T. Coleridge, D.C.L. Fifth Edition. Post 8vo., cloth, 6s.

OCCASIONAL PAPERS AND REVIEWS, on Sir Walter Scott, Poetry, and Sacred Poetry. By the late Rev. John Keble. Author of "The Christian Year." Demy 8vo., cloth extra, 12s.

Archdeacon Denison.

NOTES OF MY LIFE, 1805—1878. By George Anthony Denison, Vicar of East Brent, 1845: Archdeacon of Taunton, 1851. Third Edition, 8vo., cloth, 12s.

Bishop Herbert de Losinga.

THE FOUNDER OF NORWICH CATHEDRAL. The LIFE, LETTERS, and SERMONS of BISHOP HERBERT DE LOSINGA (b. circ. A.D. 1050, d. 1119). By Edward Meyrick Goulburn, D.D., Dean of Norwich, and Henry Symonds, M.A. 2 vols., 8vo., cloth, 30s.

John Armstrong.

LIFE OF JOHN ARMSTRONG, D.D., late Lord Bishop of Grahamstown. By the Rev. T. T. Carter, M.A., Rector of Clewer. Third Edition. Fcap. 8vo., with Portrait, cloth, 7s. 6d.

Bishop Wilson.

THE LIFE OF THE RIGHT REVEREND FATHER IN GOD, THOMAS WILSON, D.D., Lord Bishop of Sodor and Man. By the late Rev. John Keble, M.A., Vicar of Hursley. 2 vols., 8vo., cloth, £1 1s.

THE SAINTLY LIFE OF MRS. MARGARET GODOLPHIN. 16mo., 1s.

FOOTPRINTS ON THE SANDS OF TIME. Biographies for Young People. Fcap., limp cloth, 2s. 6d.

THE AUTHORIZED EDITIONS OF

THE CHRISTIAN YEAR,

With the Author's latest Corrections and Additions.

NOTICE.—Messrs. PARKER are the sole Publishers of the Editions of the "Christian Year" issued with the sanction and under the direction of the Author's representatives. All Editions without their imprint are unauthorized.

Handsomely printed on toned *s. d.* paper. SMALL 4to. EDITION.		32mo. EDITION.	*s. d.*
Cloth extra . . . 10 6		Cloth, limp 1 0	
		Cloth boards, gilt edges . 1 6	
DEMY 8vo. EDITION. Cloth 6 0		48mo. EDITION.	
		Cloth, limp 0 6	
FCAP. 8vo. EDITION. Cloth 3 6		Roan 1 6	
		FACSIMILE OF THE 1ST EDI-	
24mo. EDIT. With red lines, cl. 2 6		TION. 2 vols., 12mo., boards 7 6	

The above Editions are kept in a variety of bindings.

By the same Author.

LYRA INNOCENTIUM. Thoughts in Verse on Christian Children. *Thirteenth Edition.* Fcap. 8vo., cloth, 5s.
————— 48mo. edition, limp cloth, 6d. ; cloth boards, 1s.
MISCELLANEOUS POEMS by the Rev. JOHN KEBLE, M.A., Vicar of Hursley. *Third Edition.* Fcap. cloth, 6s.
THE PSALTER OR PSALMS OF DAVID : In English Verse. *Fourth Edition.* Fcap., cloth, 6s.

The above may also be had in various bindings.

By the late Rev. ISAAC WILLIAMS.

THE CATHEDRAL ; or, The Catholic and Apostolic Church in England. Fcap. 8vo., cloth, 5s.; 32mo., cloth, 2s. 6d.
THE BAPTISTERY ; or, The Way of Eternal Life. Fcap. 8vo., cloth, 7s. 6d. (with the Plates) ; 32mo., cloth, 2s. 6d.
HYMNS translated from the PARISIAN BREVIARY. 32mo., cloth, 2s. 6d.
THE CHRISTIAN SCHOLAR. Fcap. 8vo., cloth, 5s. ; 32mo., cloth, 2s. 6d.
THOUGHTS IN PAST YEARS. 32mo., cloth, 2s. 6d.
THE SEVEN DAYS ; or, The Old and New Creation. Fcap. 8vo., cloth, 3s. 6d.

CHRISTIAN BALLADS AND POEMS.

By ARTHUR CLEVELAND COXE, D.D., Bishop of Western New York. A New Edition, printed in Red and Black, Fcap. 8vo., cloth, 2s. 6d.—Cheap Edition, 1s.

The POEMS of GEORGE HERBERT.

THE TEMPLE. Sacred Poems and Private Ejaculations. A New Edition, in Red and Black, 24mo., cloth 2s. 6d.—Cheap Edition, 1s.

THE ARCHBISHOP OF CANTERBURY.

SINGLEHEART. By Dr. EDWARD WHITE BENSON, Archbishop of Canterbury, late Bishop of Truro, &c. ADVENT SERMONS, 1876, preached in Lincoln Cathedral. Second Edition. Crown 8vo., cloth, 2s. 6d.

THE BISHOP OF SALISBURY.

UNIVERSITY SERMONS ON GOSPEL SUBJECTS. By the Right Rev. the LORD BISHOP OF SALISBURY. Fcap. 8vo., cl., 2s. 6d.

THE BISHOP OF NEWCASTLE.

THE AWAKING SOUL. As sketched in the 130th Psalm. Addresses delivered at St. Peter's, Eaton-square, on the Tuesdays in Lent, 1877, by E. R. WILBERFORCE, M.A. [Rt. Rev. the Lord Bp. of Newcastle]. Crown 8vo., limp cloth, 2s. 6d

THE LATE BISHOP OF SALISBURY.

SERMONS ON THE BEATITUDES, with others mostly preached before the University of Oxford ; to which is added a Preface relating to the volume of "Essays and Reviews." New Edition. Crown 8vo., cloth, 7s. 6d.

THE BISHOP OF BARBADOS.

SERMONS PREACHED ON SPECIAL OCCASIONS. By JOHN MITCHINSON, D.D., late Bishop of Barbados. Crown 8vo., cloth, 5s.

VERY REV. THE DEAN OF CHICHESTER.

SHORT SERMONS FOR FAMILY READING, following the Course of the Christian Seasons. By Very Rev. J. W. BURGON, B.D., Dean of Chichester. First Series. 2 vols., Fcap. 8vo., cloth, 8s.
—— SECOND SERIES. 2 vols., Fcap. 8vo., cloth, 8s.

REV. J. KEBLE.

SERMONS, OCCASIONAL AND PAROCHIAL. By the late Rev. JOHN KEBLE, M.A., Vicar of Hursley. 8vo., cloth, 12s.

THE REV. CANON PAGET.

THE REDEMPTION OF WORK. ADDRESSES spoken in St. Paul's Cathedral, by FRANCIS PAGET, M.A., Senior Student of Christ Church, Oxford. 52 pp. Fcap. 8vo., cloth, 2s.

CONCERNING SPIRITUAL GIFTS. Three Addresses to Candidates for Holy Orders in the Diocese of Ely. With a Sermon. By FRANCIS PAGET, M.A., Senior Student of Christ Church, Oxford. Fcap. 8vo., cloth, 2s. 6d.

THE REV. CANON HOLE.

HINTS TO PREACHERS, ILLUSTRATED BY SERMONS AND ADDRESSES. By S. REYNOLDS HOLE, Canon of Lincoln. Second Edition. Post 8vo., cloth, 6s.

𝔚orks of the Standard English Divines,

PUBLISHED IN THE LIBRARY OF ANGLO-CATHOLIC THEOLOGY.

Andrewes' (Bp.) Complete Works. 11 vols., 8vo., £3 7s.
THE SERMONS. (Separate.) 5 vols., £1 15s.

Beveridge's (Bp.) Complete Works. 12 vols., 8vo., £4 4s.
THE ENGLISH THEOLOGICAL WORKS. 10 vols., £3 10s.

Bramhall's (Abp.) Works, with Life and Letters, &c.
5 vols., 8vo., £1 15s.

Bull's (Bp.) Harmony on Justification. 2 vols., 8vo., 10s.

———————— **Defence of the Nicene Creed.** 2 vols., 10s.

———————— **Judgment of the Catholic Church.** 5s.

Cosin's (Bp.) Works Complete. 5 vols., 8vo., £1 10s.

Crakanthorp's Defensio Ecclesiæ Anglicanæ. 8vo., 7s.

Frank's Sermons. 2 vols., 8vo., 10s.

Forbes' Considerationes Modestæ. 2 vols., 8vo., 12s.

Gunning's Paschal, or Lent Fast. 8vo., 6s.

Hammond's Practical Catechism. 8vo., 5s.

———————— **Miscellaneous Theological Works.** 5s.

———————— **Thirty-one Sermons.** 2 Parts. 10s.

Hickes's Two Treatises on the Christian Priesthood.
3 vols., 8vo., 15s.

Johnson's (John) Theological Works. 2 vols., 8vo., 10s.

———————— **English Canons.** 2 vols., 12s.

Laud's (Abp.) Complete Works. 7 vols., (9 Parts,) 8vo.,
£2 17s.

L'Estrange's Alliance of Divine Offices. 8vo., 6s.

Marshall's Penitential Discipline. 8vo., 4s.

Nicholson's (Bp.) Exposition of the Catechism. (This
volume cannot be sold separate from the complete set.)

Overall's (Bp.) Convocation-book of 1606. 8vo., 5s.

Pearson's (Bp.) Vindiciæ Epistolarum S. Ignatii.
2 vols., 8vo., 10s.

Thorndike's (Herbert) Theological Works Complete.
6 vols., (10 Parts,) 8vo., £2 10s.

Wilson's (Bp.) Works Complete. With Life, by Rev.
J. KEBLE. 7 vols., (8 Parts,) 8vo., £3 3s.

     * * *The 81 Vols. in 88, for £15 15s. net.*

CHEAPER ISSUE OF TALES FOR YOUNG MEN »
AND WOMEN. ·ſ,

In Six Half-crown Vols., in handsome and attractive cloth
bindings, suitable for School Prizes and Presents.

Vol. I. contains Mother and Son, Wanted a Wife, and Hobson's Choice, by the Rev. F. E. PAGET.

Vol. II. Wyndecote Hall, Squitch, Tenants at Tinkers' End,
by the Rev. F. E. PAGET.

Vol. III. Two Cottages, The Sisters, and Old Jarvis's Will,
by the Rev. W. E. HEYGATE.

Vol. IV. James Bright the Shopman, The Politician, Irre-
vocable, by the Rev. W. E. HEYGATE.

Vol. V. The Strike, and Jonas Clint, by the Rev. R. KING ;
Two to One, and False Honour, by the Rev. N. BROWN.

Vol. VI. Railway Accident, by the Rev. J. M. NEALE ;
The Recruit, Susan, Servants' Influence, Mary Thomas, or Dis-
sent at Evenly, by the Rev. E. MONRO ; Caroline Elten, or
Vanity and Jealousy, by the Rev. H. HAYMAN.

Each Volume is bound as a distinct work, and sold separately.

The late Dr. Elvey's Psalter.

Just published, 16mo., cloth, 1s. ; by Post, 1s. 2d.

A CHEAP EDITION (being the 16th) of

THE PSALTER ; or, Canticles and Psalms of David.

Pointed for Chanting on a New Principle. With Explanations
and Directions. By the late STEPHEN ELVEY, Mus. Doc.,
Organist of New and St. John's Colleges, and Organist and ·
Choragus to the University of Oxford. With a Memorandum
on the Pointing of the *Gloria Patri*, by Sir G. J. ELVEY.

Also,

II. FCAP. 8vo. EDITION (the 14th), limp cloth, 2s. 6d.
With PROPER PSALMS. 3s.

III. LARGE TYPE EDITION for ORGAN (the 8th).
Demy 8vo., cloth, 5s.

THE PROPER PSALMS separately. Fcap. 8vo., sewed, 6d.

THE CANTICLES separately (17th Edition). Fcap. 8vo., 3d.

The Psalter is used at St. George's Chapel, Windsor, and at many Cathedrals·

"There can be no doubt but that we owe most of what is good in the
chanting of to-day to the (seven years') labour and care bestowed on the first
edition of this work issued in 1856."—*Musical Standard, Sept.* 25, 1875.

"Taken as a whole, Dr. Elvey's work has not been surpassed. . . . We
believe that educated musicians generally—with a sense of the importance
of this part of worship—if they must chant !rom such a pointed Psalter,
would prefer Dr. Elvey's conscientious framework to any other we know."—
The Orchestra, January, 1878.